UNCONDITIONAL
LOVE

UNCONDITIONAL
LOVE

*CONDITIONS APPLY

ATHIRATH VIJAY REDDY

PARTRIDGE

To order additional copies of this book, contact
Partridge India
000 800 10062 62
orders.india@partridgepublishing.com

www.partridgepublishing.com/india

Contents

Foreword

This book is dedicated to my dad and the greatest guy we lost
Vijay bhaskar reddy.

Im proud to be Athirath vijay reddy. You have lived all your life, protecting us, providing us, carrying us on your shoulders. I wish I coulld be 1/100th of what you are. Even I write a million books like this or make my way to the moon and back I can't be a bigger man than you are.

To the greatest man on earth who stays in heaven all I can say is I love you. We miss you and I can never say thank you because it's too little to say for everything you did for us.

The only unconditional love we ever felt was the love you've showered on us. I couldn't do anything for you dad but I promise to keep your name high for as long as I live, the only gift I could give to you.

We know you are still watching us, protecting us loving us.

Thank you mom, kavitha reddy for believing in me even in the times when I couldn't believe in myself.

Thank you for loving us.

Thank you for taking care of us.

Thank you for being the best mother in world.

I can never say this out loud to you but I love you mom.

Vicky a.k.a. abhimanyu reddy thank you for being the kid/elder brother.

Thanks for reading the book million times after every rough draft and listening to the narration billion times before the book was on paper. I cant ask for a better brother than you.

Akshay you owe me million so I wont say thank you but I sure miss you from the day you left hyderabad. Comeback jack ass or ill drag you down here. My best friend for this life time.

Thank you haseena for being there in my highs and lows my longest and sweetest friend from the other gender.

Abhinay, vamshi I cant thank you guys enough for getting this book on board.

Thank you for being there always. Thank you for eventually you've done for me. If it wasn't for you guys this book woould have still been in my shelf.

The first guy who said this book is "awesome" chandu. Actually thank you divya for reading the book and passing the message on to me through chandu. I know chandu didn't read even a single page.

I owe you a lot nausheen for bringing the words in to a harmony of music. Thank you for proof reading my book and lying so hard that I'm better than chetan bhagat

Prologue

The year is 1980; those were the days when the word city was not included in the dictionary of India. It's a beautiful evening, the sun is about to set and the last glow of sun is illuminating the light house up above the hill. The light house is an old construction. The white color on the light house looked pale and was marked at several places with love symbols and names of many young lovers. The wooden doors were weak and made sounds every time wind blew. The light house is flanked by a beautiful beach on one side and a deserted road on the other leading to a hill. The light house has no visitors other than birds nesting here or in rare cases young couples who hunt for a quite place away from everyone's eyes, but that day there is no one around. Surya was sitting on the third step from the bottom, with his feet resting on the first step and his elbows on his knees. His hands were sweaty and he kept fidgeting. He looked nervous and scared but he kept his heart positive though. He is wearing a white shirt and khaki pants the only good dress that was borrowed from Vijay his best friend. There is a passageway at the center facing the large wooden doors, paved with cobblestone. Both sides of the path have a garden of grass and wild orchids, which unattended grew up to the height of his knees. The place is beautiful, wildly beautiful. All this stuff never registered in Surya's head. He kept looking at the far end of the road; His eyes were waiting for something on the road ahead of him.

The sun dissolved into the water of the lake leaving behind the darkness. Surya is still sitting there, his eyes still waiting for something. He then saw a bright light at the far end of the road, traveling right towards him. This light turned out to be a white ambassador. That car slowed down as it approached the light house. It stopped right in front of the light house. Surya's heart beat gained pace as the car approached the light house and stopped in front of the light house.

Thirty seconds later when the silence was all around the place, Ahalya stepped out of the car and walked towards Surya. Ahalya was wearing a white gown which stretched up to her feet. Surya stood up and his heart started beating fast as she walked up to him. His eyes started glowing with joy. As she walked closer to him his eyes fell on the big shinning stone on the wedding finger of ahalya. His heart filled with tears when he saw that. His strong knees felt week, he fell down on his back at the second step. His head bowed down along with his shoulders to hide tears. She walked further towards him and fell down on her knees. Tears started dropping out of her eyes. The silence was still engulfing the place. She dropped down to her knees on the floor and covered her face with her hands. Few moments later Surya stood up and walked up to her. He kneeled down in front of her, held Ahalya's head around the neck and wiped her tears with his thumbs.

Surya controlled his tears and said in a firm voice "don't cry, it's ok."

Ahalya tried to speak but her words couldn't line up with her tears. Finally Surya held her by shoulders and lifted her up. He kissed her on the forehead. His hands started to fall back, she caught them between her hands relenting to let go. Surya shedding a few tears took his hands back and said "go". She looked up, as he made a small twinkle of a smile at his lips and said "I still love you, now you have to go". Surya then turned back to hide his tears.

Ahalya stood there sobbing for few seconds to look at Surya one last time but he didn't turn back. Skies started to wail in grief in the form of rain. Ahalya hugged Surya tightly one last time from the back and walked back faster sobbing. Surya stood there heartbroken.

The next day Ahalya's car stopped in front of Surya's house in the village. Surya's house was in the working sector of the village. The compound wall of the house is short and broken at few places in the outside. There is a rusted iron gate opening to the muddy pathway which leads to a long porch with grills and another iron gate. Large group of men are standing in three to four sets in the garden area of the house. It's the first car they ever saw for most of them. Ahalya stepped out of the car wearing a white sari with gold pallu and her sleeves stretched up to her forearm. She dragged her sari's pallu in the damp of previous night rain carelessly and opened the rusted Iron Gate.

There were large group of women standing in the porch who turned their heads towards Ahalya as the gate made a squeaking sound. All the women started whispering and staring at Ahalya through the grill. Ahalya expressed no remark towards them.

She passed through the flat stones in the middle and the steps to enter the house. She was deprived of the finesse and grace she used to possess, when she passed through the steel gate of balcony. She turned lifeless when she opened the wooden door to enter the house.

The house is filled with people squalling, wailing in grief there is Surya's dad sobbing silently life less. There was his mother wailing with her hair gone loose. All other women are trying to console her. There was his best friend Vijay silently sobbing at one corner, but her eyes couldn't note anything else but Surya lying in the middle of unroofed part of the house under the sun. She started to approach Surya with no life in her knees when vijay saw her from a corner. He passed through all the relatives wiping his tears, caught Ahalya by her shoulder and dragged her out of the house. Vijay threw Ahalya on the closed back door of the car and turned towards the house.

Ahalya recovered and turned towards Vijay sobbing and said 'Vijay please....'

Vijay turned back at Ahalya shedding tears, said 'don't...'

Vijay took a pause to control his tears and wiped his face.

'He loved you Ahalya and you killed him, now leave.'

'Vijay please let me see him one last time. Please let me cry for him Ahalya said wailing. 'No ahalya you don't get to see him. You don't deserve that...'

'Vijay PLEASE' Ahalya wailed in a loud screeching voice as Vijay walked away from her.

Vijay went into the house and closed the gate behind him Ahalya dropped down to her feet wailing in grief.

Chapter 1

The beginning

Vijay is sitting under a tree. He is a strong guy who was born to the Zamindar pratap of that village; He had two brothers and three sisters. His eldest brother konda left the village to pursue his dream to be a revenue officer for the government. The one after that Venkat and Vijay are the only ones in the village. Vijay is the last son, but the strongest son in the family. He is tall and has huge shoulders but he still has a charm of a kid. His thick mustache and sharp eyes made him look like his father Zamindar Pratap. He could entice anybody and everybody in the village with his words. He also had a strong heart the one that could stop the world if it had to. Everyone in the village thought Vijay would go places with his persona, but all he ever wanted is to follow his mother's footsteps. He wanted to work in the farm; he wanted to take care of the cattle.

As he looked into the sky he remembered the story his mother used to say when he was a kid. He still remembers it as yesterday. His mom after a laborious day in the field used to make Vijay sit in her lap serve food in a plate and tell this while feeding him with her hands

1

"Once upon a time there was a Zamindar, he had three sons. All three of them stayed as a family until Zamindar got bedridden and died. Zamindar was the wealthiest guy in those times. The land of zamindar stretched till the far end of the village. The cattle of Zamindar were huge enough to feed all the villages nearby. The last son of Zamindar Pratap got less than one third of the property and accepted it gracefully. As it is enough to last till generations but he had 3 daughters and as the days passed daughters in the family took a huge part of the property with them to their in-laws houses. Pratap also had three sons the last two were less than ten years when he demised with tuberculosis. All the other brothers of Pratap doomed as well. Now Zamindar's family name is lost in the ages of time."

Zamindar pratap passed away when vijay was five years old.

As he woke up from the trance he felt heavy in the heart. His best friend and his only friend was no more. Surya is one whom you can call the one with the heart of gold. Unlike vijay, surya was born in a middle class family. He was the son of the school head master. So every time vijay missed his school surya would cover his attendance in the register. One time when he was doing that he got caught but he didn't take vijay's name. His own father rusticated him from the school that day. From that day Vijay and surya are not two different people they are one. Vijay finished his studies and joined his brother in farming. Surya on the other hand joined the sugar factory on the outskirts as a worker. The owner of the sugar factory brought his daughter ahalya along with him sometimes. Surya being the finest among the workers owner asked him to be as the guide for her as long as she is in the factory. Ahalya had a crush on surya since their childhood since they all went to the only school in the village. She knew everything about surya from his wake up timings to his food and drinking habits. She made him carry food cooked from her house, which she later used to order him to eat. She also made him dress up in new clothes which surya was not used to. Surya unwillingly complied for everything as she was his boss's daughter but one day he resisted. Ahalya then apologized to him and expressed her love. Later surya got so used to her that, it became a ritual for him to sleep resting his head in ahalya's lap after a long laborious day in factory

Then one day ahalya's father came to know about them. He didn't lock her in the house like any other father. All he said is she could go to Surya any day but he said "that day would be his last day". Surya tried to contact her several times but she was bound by her father's words. Surya one day sneaked into her palace and confronted her. They both embraced each other. At that moment she forgot everything, her father and the promises she made to him. She promised surya that she would elope and marry him on the wedding day. so he was waiting at the light house but that day she saw her father at the last step out of her house from the back door. Her father's was chatting with his friends with a glass of imported wine in his hands; she saw that he was happy. She then had a vision of the future. She knew that her father wouldn't last an hour after he knew that her daughter eloped. She had to choose, but she never thought surya would…..

Since then Vijay started hating love; he never let anyone come close to his heart. Even if he did he never expressed.

He stood up and looked at the setting sun on the other side of the lake. It's been hours since he came here. He lined up the cattle grazing around the lake and started walking towards the house behind the cattle. His head went back into a trance as he walked. He remembered the days where Vijay and Surya used to role tires in the childhood. He remembered the afternoons where they used to bunk school to catch a film in the town theatre. He remembered the evenings when they laughed their guts out under the banyan tree looking at the villagers talk and fight at the Panchayat. He missed Surya a lot, it's like a piece of him had left him that day.

As he walked towards the house he saw his brother throwing his clothes filled in a suitcase out of the house, His mother yelling and sobbing on the right side of the veranda.

Venkat looked at Vijay as he stood there behind the cattle. He rushed towards his stuff, as some of them had memories of Surya in them. He picked all the stuff that reminded him of surya and kept them inside the suitcase. He then looked at Venkat standing at the higher step of the front door.

"Where have you been since afternoon" Venkat shouted.

Vijay looked at venkat in his eyes

"I took the cattle out for grazing and I fell asleep under the tree".

'You worthless piece of shit, you do nothing all day and now you are lying too. You were drinking all day at the liquor store. There are 15 rupees missing in the house.' Venkat still shouting in feigned anger

'I never touched liquor in my life and I never would. The fifteen rupees I took from mother is true. I gave it to Surya's family they are poor and their only son is...

"Who do you think you are to give money to charity? You worthless junk, you sit all day at the house and now you started throwing money at beggars'.

'SHUT UP". Vijay roared at his brother as he became red with anger. There was silence all over.

'You have no right to talk about them. This money is not your money, it's mine too. You didn't earn it we inherited it'

"GETOUT, GETOUT of the house now."

"You always wanted him to leave the house. My elder son already left and now if he leaves you can have all this wealth for yourself." Vijay's mother wailed as Vijay started packing his stuff on the floor.

"Mother that's ok let him have it. I'll go and stay with Konda", Vijay smiled at her with his eyes welled up.

Vijay started walking away. The cattle with which he spent the most of his time with started howling in the sadness. Venkat took the stick Vijay left and started hitting them.

Vijay walked into the darkness that day, and that day he had a new beginning

Chapter 2

The sunny side

Year 2008

I woke up when star movies is playing in TV. Hulk is squashing the three tanks like mangoes. Shit I forgot to switch off the TV last night. I tried to search for my remote eyes closed on the bed. I opened my eyes as I couldn't find it on the bed. It's lying on the floor in three pieces. Shit again I must have kicked it out of the bed last night. I got up to sitting position and fixed it. I switched the channel at the break 10 clicks on the up button later I'm watching my favorite song of Salman "oh oh jaane jaana." On MTV, then skipped channel to Friends in W.B. and skipped it again at the break. Fifteen minutes later I couldn't remember which channel I was watching, so I paused to remember at Telebrands sauna belt add.

Knock Knock,

My mom started banging the door as hard as she can.

'What mom.' I shouted to be heard outside the room.

'Your phone had been ringing since half an hour.' My mom replied from behind the door. 'Someone named. Arun is calling again."

'Shit, shit, shit, I am coming out in 10 minutes.'

Arun is codename for Avanthika; I save my girl friend's names with a boy's name for two reasons. One girl wouldn't find out about the other even if she scrolled through my phone book, two my family would think I am still the geek I was in the childhood.

I switched the channel to M.T.V with a Jannat title song playing on the back ground; I freshen up as fast as I can. I ran out of my room with my belt hanging unbuckled and few buttons of my shirt unbuttoned. My hands are busy tucking the shirt into my pants.

"Surya Tiffin ..." my mom shouted from the kitchen.

"I don't have time mom, I am running late" I replied tying my shoelace.

'SHUT UP I won't let you out of the house if you don't have It.' my mom still shouting.

'Mom I really have to go I don't have time.' I said pretending to be serious but the smirk on my face gave it away.

My mom rushed out of kitchen catching a plate stuffed with idles. She started stuffing idles into my mouth when I was busy searching for my wallet. My mom knew where I left them but she didn't say where it is until the second idle is finished in my plate.

I rushed out of the house took my car out with my phone still ringing all the while and drove it through two lanes one left turn and right turn later I stopped my car in front of Hardwick towers. The most popular and hot girl of my college lives here. Guys in my college go rounds in these lanes sometimes to catch a glimpse of her. Amateurs, anyway I looked around to see if there is anyone watching me. My father is president of colony association, so I had to be careful.

It's been ten minutes since I had been waiting for Avanthika. Why do girls always do this? They ask u to come early and they always come late and it doesn't matter if we come early or late.

I could see her walking faster getting out of the lift. She looked like a ghost in the ghost busters, with her big eyes bigger with anger and her make up over loaded. She sat in the car and the door was not yet closed and she started yelling "what the hell is this Surya? I have a presentation today, you are late even today. I asked you to do one thing for me. I asked you to come early for once in your life."

How would that make any difference you are late too. I wanted to say that but I didn't, because fact 1: Einstein once said 'women are always right even if they are wrong.' All you could do is say sorry and move on.

"Sorry Avanthika my mom made me drop her at the temple." I patted myself for the lie I just made up.

'You will never listen to me Surya. I asked you not to fight with the seniors but you did. I asked you to come early once you didn't, you always, you always…

Fact 2: no matter what you say women wouldn't get convinced until they shoot you with all the bullets they have. Men are always the soldiers without guns in the battle field.

Avanthika waved her hand in front of me and said 'hello are you even listening to me?'

'I am, I am…aaa'

'What was I saying?'

'You were saying about…hmm about'. I looked left for hints and her face was boiling red.

'SURYYYYYYYYYYYAAAAAA'

Fifteen minutes and death of my left ear drum later we reached college just 5 min late dew to my excellent driving skills. She still had time to prepare as her roll number might be 6 or 7.She left and I unlocked my phone for updates walking towards my classroom.

Haseena uploaded a replica of Kate Winslet face portrait from titanic on what's app

On what's app

Me - nice pic but can you please zoom a little down under the neck. I can't see the pic clearly

Haseena- shut up bakwas mat karo

Me - ☺

Haseena- tu nahi sudarega (you would never change...)

Me - you know me better then everyone jaaneman (darling)

Me -TTYL, GTG, Reached my classroom, Bye

Haseena- ok bye :)

I signed off as I reached my classroom and opened the door.

"May I come in madam?"

My English lecturer took a turn and looked at me. Suddenly all eyes are on me now. She is the practical and fun teacher among everyone else; all I had to do is smile when I come late to get in.

"Surya the most regular student of my classroom please come in

I entered the classroom and walked a few steps towards Akshay's bench keeping my head down.

"I am not letting you sit until you give your today's excuse." Madam said with her hands folded and a smirk on my face.

"Madam...actually my car had broken down so I..."

"So…. Surya?"

"I had to ask someone else for lift."

"So AP 11 AE 3699 optra magnum parked right beside the canteen is not your car?

Fish I'm screwed: p

༄ ༅

"You are one lucky bastard," Akshay said after the tea break.

"Nothing like that." I said with a pat on his back and a smile on my face.

"What the fuck I thought you are screwed this time. She let you go!!!!"

all I could do is laugh it out.

Akshay is my best friend since the 7th day of my college. Akshay is five point something dark and the thinnest guy on earth. I didn't even notice him in the first seven days.

The story behind we becoming friends is really funny, He ate my lunch box before or in the lunch break. I've bashed him good keeping in mind his size

"ENOUGH" he yelled 10 minutes later.

His face was red and tears were about to drop from his eyes.

"Akshay are you hurt?" I said with a guilty smile.

I was controlling my smile his face was funny. There was no reply from akshay.

"Akshay lets have coke in canteen my treat."

"Let's go" akshay said and got up.

We went to the canteen with few other friends I bought coke for all of them, and he roasted me and other friends in the classroom. By the end of lunch break we became best of friends

That day we laughed our brains out and since that day he always shares my box and lot more we are best friends forever.

Chapter 3

Elder/kid brother...

Surya has a kid brother named Vicky and surya loves him. Vicky is a fat kid next door. The guy girls wouldn't notice all their life. He was arjun kapoor on the fat days. He had a few good features such as his height and dimples but those were demolished due to lack of construction on his other body parts. he has a very small and parallel universe. He watches movies, plays video games, loves cricket playing and watching. He always says he would work out but that day never comes. He had his interests on one girl but he visualized the consequences if he hits on her as every average guy does and took the back seat.

It's a regular Monday he was sleeping in his room Vijay his father knocked on the door.

"Vicky?"

'Ya coming" he said in a sleepy voice

Vicky woke up from his sleep in his boxers and t shirt from previous day. He opened the door and crashed back on the bed facing his head up. Vijay sat on the side of a bed. He laid hand on Vicky's stomach

Vijay said "You don't have college today nana?" in a sweet tone.

"ya dad I'm running late ill get ready in a while."

"What happened between you two?"

"He asked me 10k I asked him to take less and...."

"And what dad?"

"We had an argument and he went out of the house without his bag and lunch box." Vijay said wiggling his head form left to right and shrugging his shoulders. "He is spending too much at least ask him not to go around with girls."

"Ooh you know that!" Vicky said surprised

"Everyone knows that's the topic in the walkers club these days."

"But they are just friends dad." Vicky said trying to hide the smile on his face

Vijay became irritated as he thought that both of them are playing with him and said "I'm not seven, and people won't think that way even if they are."

"Ask him not to do all this in the colony."

"You spoke to him about this?"

"Obviously not"

"So you fought with him using another weapon of yours..."

'Aah...kind off' Vijay said with a guilty smile

'Dad!!'

Vijay stood up and took money out of his right pocket and gave it to Vicky. 'Anyway here is his money don't let him know that I know.

'About what?'

'About...' Vijay said feeling embarrassed

'About??'

'I am just kidding dad.' Vicky chuckled

Vijay smiled and gave a playful pat on Vicky's stomach and left.

ʘ ʘ

Vicky is sitting in the canteen with his best friend pranthik waiting for lunch. A group of seniors walked in and stopped in front of their table.

'You and you both get up and go with him....' a senior said pointing his finger at both of them rudely.

'Pardon?' pranthik mumbled

'I asked you mother fuckers to get my luggage from the car parked over there.' Senior barked at them.

'It's funny that the only mother fucker I know is standing right in front of me.' Vicky said nonchalantly.

'What did you just say? Senior said moving towards Vicky. Vicky stood up and both of them are now facing each other. Senior accidentally stepped on Vicky's foot. Vicky pushed him away and all the other friends of him caught him from dropping down.

Senior kept barking 'you mother fuckers I guarantee you won't reach home today...' while he was taken away by his friends. During this time Vicky's phone was ringing continuously and Vicky accidentally answered his phone. The one who was calling him was sunny (me).

I heard the whole conversation and by the time the phone call was disconnected, I gathered my friends Akshay, Praneeth. Sathvik and left to his college. Praneeth is a thug in our college and also my best friend, but unlike anything you imagine about a thug as in tall and heavy praneeth is short and stout, with deep set eyes, result of liquid diet (royal

14

stag, bagpipers). And Sathvik is also a good friend of mine the escape guy we use when things go sore. Pranthik sent me his picture through BBM; I spotted him sitting with two of his friends in the college canteen. I punched his nose with knuckle duster blood started dropping out. I caught his shirt and dragged him out of the canteen wobbling left and right. A small group had gathered around us to witness the spectacle which comprised mostly of geeks and nerds from first year, his juniors. They followed us throughout the show I thought His friends would interfere but they didn't. By the time we were out of the canteen Tharamati was standing there. Tharamati is a also a thug like Praneeth. Praneeth and tharamati knew each other. we made the senior apologize, though he was looking up the whole time to stop the bleeding.

The guards in the college got hint of what was happening. Everyone over there scattered in fear of the college dean. I looked back and I found Vicky standing in the far end of the crowd.

'Are you fucking retarded!!!??' Vicky whisper screamed as the guards were right behind me.

Vicky started pacing towards the parking lot I walked right next to him parallel.

'I could have been suspended for this'

'But you didn't right' I said smiling.

'That's the reason why I didn't tell this to you. You raise your hand first and then comes your reasoning skills.'

'Sorry ra, though I took care of the senior pretty well he wouldn't dare to complain.'

'YOU STILL DON'T GET IT DO YOU!!?' Vicky yelled. What if a lecturer or a guard saw you hitting him? Then what?

'Sorry but I was careful none did.

'No I was lucky this time.'

'Sorry I promise I'll take the fight outside next time.'

Vicky stopped walking and looked at me seriously for a split second he then tried to hide his smile but he couldn't.

'You wouldn't change, don't dare to enter my college next time.' Vicky said smiling

'You don't own this college there are lots of gorgeous girls here too.' I chuckled

Vicky jumped at me trying to choke me

The next second I got hit by something really hard which took me down to the ground. By the time I recovered I knew it was a Hyundai I 10 car. I blazed towards the driver's seat and was yelling at the driver. Though I wasn't hurt I was angry because of the shock I went through. The driver was about to get punched when my brother came in and separated me from him.

I thought Vicky did this to save his ass from dean of the college but then I thought he didn't pick me up from the ground, he didn't step in during the argument with the driver. Then I saw him looking back, I saw a short girl with fair complexion stepping into the car.

'Is that swathi Ewww!!!' I said embarrassed by my brother's taste.

My loving brother was in trance all the while. He later said this to me that all he could remember is his GIRL stepping out of the car and walking towards him, Her eyes blinking, lips moving in slow motion. A hundred violins playing in the background just like a scene in (main hoon na) until the point she pointed at me catching the driver's collar.

I might puke if I have to write anything more than this about his girl.

Chapter 4

Me; dad; stupid bet

I didn't introduce myself in the beginning. I come from a Telugu south Indian family. If you consider tamilians to be orthodox, and if you consider mumbaikars modern and not so orthodox, my family falls in the middle partly orthodox and partly modern. We are based in Hyderabad city of Andhra Pradesh, The city which is famous for irani chai charminar and biryani.

My house is a penthouse of an apartment built by my dad named after my grandfather. Its around 4000 sqft with two roof gardens, big-hall with open kitchen, three bedrooms. When some one enters the hall from the main door to the left there is a dining table parallel to a small bed we call divan facing the wall mounted T.V. and wooden shelves. On the other side of the wall adjoining the diwan there is a roof garden. To the right there is a l shaped wooden sofa set adjoining a wall which also has a roof garden on the other side.

The garden on one side has a staircase made of steel which lead to the terrace above my house, which is my favorite place in the house. I go there everyday at least a walk for five minutes or for a puff.

The house is well lit and elegant unlike my room abutting the kitchen which my friends call the dumpster of the house.

The first thing anyone could notice when the enter the room is a pile of indefinite things on my bed. The pile has clothes, plates, jam, bowls, waterbootles, infinite other things. It keeps growing in size, an year from today it will touch the roof of my room. There is a tv on the left corner facing the bed and abutting attached bathroom. To the left of my bed there are three cupboards attached to the wall. When I have to sleep I move the pile little bit and make a birth similar to birth in train and sleep. My mother's ambition is to clean my room someday but I've forbidden anyone to touch my stuff.

My brother's room on the other end of the house facing the main door. His room is a little bigger than my room and it looks like heaven compared to my room, neat, clean, and boring. There is no t.v. in his room but two study tables one occupied by pile of books which are racing with my pile to the roof and the other has a computer from 2nd generation which hardly works. There are two small cupboards and a bathroom adjoining the computer desk.

Master bedroom is perpendicular to my brother's room and more spacious than all other rooms but you can find nothing other than a king size bed and two nightstands each at either corners.

Coming back to the city, hyderabad is a heaven for the people who love it. We are famous for biryani I bet if bradpitt lives here for sixmonths he will go back looking like a twin brother of jack black. Other than that we have all the other stuff a metro could have. Clubs, beautiful girls, brands, resorts you name it we have it.

We even have another good quality. People don't bother other people here. There is no shivsena which beats you up if you go out with a girl on a date like they do in mumbai. There are also no thugs who would bother you if you go out in the night like delhi. So a skinny guy like akshay or a hunk like me could go out on a date at anytime and at anyplace if he could handle little starring by people, And if you are into the cultural heritage about hyderabad feel free to google I'm not into that stuff anyway.

About me; my friends would say I am good, loving, down to earth, arrogant, and have an ego of a demigod. All this might be partially false or completely true. I am definitely not a regular guy you see every day. I am 6 foot tall, charming, handsome, headstrong, and fucking retarded if someone pisses me off. I could definitely say that I acquired this from my dad.

My dad is so head strong that he could look into god's eyes and say he doesn't give a damn. You can love him or hate him but you can never ignore him. He is like a demigod in the family and in his circle of friends; no the right term would be KING. He is a KING to everyone I know. He made billions when I was a kid coming from rags. He went into politics and lost a fortune, but still had millions in his pockets. When I meant pockets yes in his pockets, He stuffs million rupees into his pockets before he leaves home.

If anyone from person he barely knows to the friends and family has a problem first number they dial is my father's. No one dared to mess with my father dew to his political connections and his temper. The only person who had total disregard to his words was me. There is a saying that like minds collide that saying is completely true in our case. I am total replica; if not completely may be majority of my father. I think that's what made us behave the way we did. We never talk so much. Vicky is his emotional support and I am the pain in his ass. All we mostly did is fight and make up. But I know inertly he loved me more than Vicky.

Coming back to the story avanthika and me were not having an affair as the whole college thought we were. We were going out, we chatted 6 to 8 hours a day. We were both attracted to each other. Until one day.

That day I had to submit a project report on business communication, and I was late as usual. She being very sweet offered to do my work. I made a pit stop racing towards the college. I saw a dark chick with spots and holes dew to pimples all over the face and a moustache above her lips. It didn't took me long to recognize that she is Avanthika. She fooled the whole college with her makeup. Since that day there was no attraction towards her anymore. We were just friends since then, and that ruined too soon.

Few days later Ashmit a friend from my colony being a big belland that he is he took her number from my phone and texted her.

I got a call from her 'Do you know any guy named ashmit?'

'ya why?'

'What the fuck do you think of yourself? She barked

'What happened?'

'Why did you give him my number? ASSHOLE.!!!'

'I didn't'

'Don't lie jack ass'

'Shut up you could believe me or go to hell.' I yelled back at her.

I've cut the call, and that's the last time we spoke to each other. After that I've beaten shit out ashmit. No that would be lying, but ya I've kicked his ass to the ground. No that would be lying too, okay the truth is he landed a few punches on my face after a heated argument and I retorted. I was on diet for six pack and lean muscle which made me as thin as imran khan in janee tu ya jane naa. So I don't know how much affective my punches were but he struck me hard but the score was equal before others stepped in parted us.

I wasted few weeks behind avanthika. And here comes akshay the biggest jack ass. He is a good friend of mine but was the sole reason behind my life's biggest misfortune. I still wonder how my life would be if I hadn't drink that night.

One night we were both having scotch mixed with cranberry breezers in my car parked in front of a friend's place. As my car was totally tinted nobody bothered. Two bottles down the throat and we were tipsy. Vicky was In charge of driving me back home

'Damn… those chicks were hot.' Akshay said little groggy.

'Who?' me groggy too.

'The sisters…'

'u mean …aah …aah ..what were the names swaa.'

Akshay is chuckling as the berries have gone up to his head.

'Swathi and priya?'

'Ya..i wanna …' Akshay said with lust filled in his eyes ..

'Shut up …turkey salla (nymph).'

'Both you dick heads know that I love swathi right?' said vicky

'Dude you don't love Swathi. You just have CRUSH ON HER!!!' I yelled, I do that when I'm tipsy.

'Yeah EXACTLY!!'Akshay joined.

'Ok firstly you guys know nothing about love. Secondly stop YELLING!!

DICK HEADS!!'

'Look who is talking my little virgin brother' I said and kissed him on his cheek.

We took the bottom's up on 4th bottle sniggering at my brother.

'Every girl is not like your girl friends.' Vicky vexed.

'Oh yeah… I bet I could… One of them…

ᘉ   ᘔ

The next day morning

'God my head feels like a minefield.'

'Good for you.' My brother mumbled looking away.

I wondered why my brother was sarcastic. Akshay was snoring right next to me with his mouth open on the bed, then it struck me what I said last night.

'Fuck, I'm really sorry for what I said last night.' I apologized.

'No don't apologize the bet is on.' Vicky said sulky

'I said I'm sorry.

'Why are you chickening out?'

I got pissed

'You do realize that one of them means it could be your girl'

'aha…I do, I do. I would also like to see you fail…'

Chapter 5

The cold war

Hmm priya is definitely prettier than swathi but both looked a little similar. Priya is fair short petite girl with thick black long hair, but she was not my type. I preferred someone with long legs and great boobs someone like Sunny Leone or Katrina Kaif being highly optimistic☺. Priya was a little close to Jessica Alba in all ways.

It was a regular day; I was passing by the Panipuri stall on the corner of the Shivam Street near my house. My eyes rolled on to Swathi and Priya having Panipuri at the stall. Akshay was sleeping over so he accompanied me from college.

I harked back to the bet I had with my brother. I turned the car around and parked at the stall.

'Kaisey hoon beta? (How are you son?)' Chacha from the stall greeted me. My father is the president of the colony so people greet me where ever I go.

'Theek hoon chacha aap kaise hoon? (I'm good what about you?)' Chacha gave me and Akshay two cups with onions.

I looked from the corner of my eye and I could see that Swathi whispered into Priya's ears. I had a quick look and both of them are looking straight at me. I smiled and Swathi looked at me like a Godzilla. Priya on the other hand gave a sweet little smile.

Whenever we think we are next to god as in unbeatable, god has his own way to make us look dumb. I had third panipuri and had a sneeze the fluid rolled up to my nostrils. I touched my head and it's in my eyes too. The chilies made my eyes burn and I was jumping like a King Kong up and down with my eyes closed.

'Kya hua beta?(what happened son?)' Chacha tried to hold me but nobody can control King Kong.

Someone gave me a fresh water bottle to wash my eyes. I washed my eyes and there was priya standing to my left and Swathi behind her.

'Thank you.' I was embarrassed, I gave her bottle back.

'You are welcome.' She smiled.

They walked few steps away and started chuckling. Akshay started chuckling and even Chacha from the stall was smiling preparing pav for other customers.

ର ଛ

Few weeks later I was bored surfing the net and opened Facebook. I browsed through one of my friend's page and I noticed he liked one of swathi's photographs. I was embarrassed but I braced myself and clicked on Swathi's profile. No one knows this but I used to be petrified by swathi's name. She actually has a reputation of slapping few of her gawking admirers. So I've sent the friend request to Priya the sweet sister. My friend request got accepted immediately and she was online.

Me:Hey'

Priya:Hey'

Me:Wassup gorgeous'

Priya:Nothing much, you?'

Me:Me?! I'm doing major in Air force.'

Priya:I didn't get you I thought you were in...'

Me:You know we go where the wind blows.'I know P.J but girls like this stupid P.Js.

Priya: LOL, Then I'm captain in Air force.'

Few stupid P.Js and emojis later ...

Hey buzz me on my number (9533658536) my brother wants the P.C.

That move always worked.

We chatted for few weeks 100 P.Js and 50 flirty messages later the day has come. Akshay is on my left and Vicky is on my right with grimaced face. This was the battle between brothers. My brother and I were having cold war since a month now. We were like the countries America and Russia before the rocky IV (which ended the cold war). Rocky went for the last punch; I've hit the send button.

-'let's go out for a movie this weekend?' I've sent the message and was waiting for a reply.

1 minute passed

We were still looking at the phone screen

5 minutes passed;

We were still looking at the phone

'Do you guys need anything to ea..?' my mom barged into my room.

MOM PLEASE LEAVE, WE ARE BUSY, GO!!!!! We yelled in chorus.

10 minutes passed

I and akshay are playing WWE on P.S.2 and Vicky is working on P.C.

My phone beeped

All of us jumped on the phone pushing each other and snatching it from each other's hands, my brother got hold of it.

'YES, YES… F&*K YOU DICK HEADS!!!' he yelled pointing finger at us and jumped up in the air like a monkey with a banana.

Our faces turned pale with no color he yelled 'YES YES F&*K YOU!!! Again me and akshay looked at each other with the face Rocky would have if he lost the match with the Russian guy. We could do nothing about it Russia had won and there was no rematch.

'Sorry darling I don't go out much.' Sweetest way of saying piss off.

The consolation prize is the booty call I got that night right after the message, and I sang eye of the tiger thrice that night☺.

ℭℛ   ℬℐ

'Shut up and say sorry' haseena ordered

'Why should I do, he started it.' I protested.

If there is one girl who had power over both of us after my mother she is haseena. She is like an elder sister we never had. Whenever we have a fight she was the one we go to, to get things resolved. We weren't talking to each other since a very long time. So both of us called her and said our sides of the story and both parties were summoned by the court on a Saturday evening to banjara hills café coffee day.

'You made fun about me' Vicky complained to her.

'I was drunk' I yelled at him.

'So you could call names.'

'I said sorry the next morning.'

'SO!' '....CALLED ME DICK...!!' '....YOU WERE AFTER MY GIRL..!!' '...I DIDN'T!!.' both of us were screaming on the top our voice.

'MAM!! You guys have to leave if you don't behave.' Waitress whisper screamed at us.

We calmed down and braced ourself.

'Stop it!! Both of you' hassena whisper screamed.

'Surya is an asshole we all know that, you should have said he is an asshole and take the bet off.'

'Hey' I said looking at her sipping the strawberry shake and a frown on my forehead.

'Yes you are the biggest asshole I know. You called Vicky names and you placed a bet on Vicky's girlfriend.'

'I didn't I tried to take her sister on a date.' I said condescending.

'That's disgusting too.' She looked at me with big eyes like the father of my ex girlfriend. 'NOW SAY SORRY TO HIM!!' She whisper screamed.

'Sorry.' I mumbled

'I didn't hear you'

'I said I'm sorry okay.'

'Now hug each other..'

'ewwww no way we aren't gay.' We said in chorus.

'Worth a try...'

ℂℛ 𝔰𝔬

Chapter 6

The lucky shirt

It was one of my breakup parties, and I had a lot of drinks that night. I didn't had to worry my brother was hosting it in our house. My parents were on a trip to tirupathi and we voluntarily skipped it for sweet taste of freedom.

'That's it' I had the bottom's up of the drink in my glass. 'I'm done with woman.' I said a little buffed.

'Yeah right pigs are gonna fly.' Akshay said rolling his eyes away.

'You don't think I CAN DO IT!!' I bawled

'stop SCREAMING!!' my brother yelled 'every time.'

'I'm serious. That was my last relationship your honor.' I was sloshed by then. I got up raising my hand up pledging. 'your honor of this court of the milkway, I Surya solem... solemom..so..lemonly take an oath that I will no longer pur.. purse..pursuve girls and will put my whole energy into my dream of becoming a filmmmmaker. I started stumbling and my brother caught me

'Yeah yeah shut up now.'my sober brother held my hand around his shoulders and took me to my room.

I looked up at my brother on right and the roof 'why your honor why.. I do.. not plead guilty'

He kept saying 'okay okay' and covered me with a blanket.

'There is no place for justice... justice... just.. ice' my bawls went lower and lower and I passed out.

The next day I got up when my brother was paying home delivery guy for lunch. We never use dinner table. We sat on the dinner table for the 7th time in our life as far as i can count.

'Do you remember what you said last night?' he asked

'What?' I said baffled.

'You said you are going to get serious from today.'

'Not now, no lectures today' I protested 'I have a hangover...'

You have it every alternate day surya; you need to get your ducks in line. You see my life is simple. I would do my masters and get settled in a job, simple and you don't have a plan and you have a most unrealistic dream to be a film maker and you don't even know where to start.

'I do, I watch films all the time.' I said trying to assuage the conversation.

He looked at me as if I walked in without knocking the door while he is masturbating.

'Okay... sorry go on'

'You have to start now if you want to follow your dream or dad is going to drag you into the family business and you have to make your peace with it for the rest of your life.' He said with a stern voice and walked away.

It wasn't the first time for me to take lectures from my dad, Vicky and haseena but that day it suddenly clicked me somewhere.

I went into my room and locked myself and started writing the script for my short film, my parents thought I was sick and stopped bothering me as I yelled when someone knocked on my door. I wasn't afraid of attendance as the H.O.D was a little bit afraid about my reputation. I completed the script after one and half week and came out of the room yelling 'YES YES DONE IT!!' with a beard and smelling like a hobo. My unlucky parents had to introduce me to their guests that day in that state who came to invite us to their housewarming party, that was the last time they ever stepped into our house.

The short film is a story about a girl who is best friend of a boy since childhood and who secretly loved him. They both have a common best friend rocky. Rocky sets the girl with another boy on a fake date to make boy jealous and it works out boy realizes he loves the girl too…happy ending.

The next day I got the D.O.P for the film, I also gathered my associate directors for the film and we finalized the camera cannon 5D for 5000 per day and the stage was set but there was a small hitch.

'There was no how should I put this, there was no girl to play the lead role in the movie.' I said sipping black coffee in banjara hills coffee day.

'Wow you always outwit yourself with your dumb brain, you wrote a script with a female lead in it and you don't have a girl to play that part.' She said mocking me. She took a long pause to think. 'Beg one of your ex-girlfriends.'

'I and Vicky looked at each other with raised eyebrows.

'You don't have a single girl who is your friend except me.' Haseena said with her eyes wide open 'God I feel sorry…'

'Aww.. That's ok Haseena…' I smirked

'Not for you dick head.. for me..'she said ruefully

Akshay and Vicky laughed out loud as I laid back with a frown on my forehead.

'Why don't you ask one of your ex-girlfriends?' Vicky asked earnestly

'Hmm…Let me think one of them tried to cast a spell on me, other one unleashed her dog behind me, the last one tried to kill me and…. the one before that wanted to staple my balls to my face…the one…

Eww SHUT UP!!They said in chorus.

'I can never have this Latte in my life.' Haseena said throwing it away. I smiled and shrugged

  C3 80

Being sober when all your friends are drinking is boring so I kept myself out of hanging with lots of other friends except akshay. It was a Saturday evening I laid on my bed and started scrolling through all my contacts to find a girl for the part. As I scrolled through one of the contact, the only ex-girlfriend who wouldn't kill me on site Meera (Meera Sharma). I reminisced the conversation we had over a cup of coffee post breakup.

She looked into my eyes and said 'The problem with you is you are just a grown up baby.' She was being earnest. 'The good part about that is you can't lie even if you want to, you never speak badly about a person behind his back, you are very loyal boyfriend but the part is you are you.'

'What do you mean by that?' I smirked though I was a little bewildered by that statement.

'I don't know if I could rely on you or not, 9 out of 10 times you wouldn't do the thing I want you to do or I asked you to do. Once in a while you turn up with bruises on your face and to top it all you have ego of a Greek god. What I mean is every girl needs her guy to be stable predictable, once in a while to do something for her.'

'Okay let me interrupt you here.' I was always there for you.

'Yes you were there but relationship is just not that. When was the last time you bought me flowers?' I looked at the roof diagonally trying to think.

'See, when was the last time you came to a date on time?'

'This I did, we went for the film… what was that? Love aaj kal.

'You canceled that thrice and you were thirty five minutes late for the movie' she had a frown on the forehead. She suddenly turned angry somehow. I still wonder what ticked her off. I kept silent with a guilty smile.

'Thanks for the coffee Surya and good bye.'

I smiled and shook hands with her and looked at her as she walked away. I wanted to say a lot that day, I wanted to say I sometimes forget things okay may be all the time, that's because I have a bad memory, I sometimes don't think before I act. That doesn't mean I ever took her for granted. The bruises part was true I have a low level of patience. I hit if someone misbehaves with me or my friends. I would do the same if someone misbehaved with her too. I actually did that too. I bashed up two guys for misbehaving with her in a coffee shop, she was shell shocked that day. She took a promise from me not to get into fight anymore, I broke that promise next month.

I exhaled a long breath and scrolled down. I found one contact Priya, The only girl who turned me down. I decided to ask her but I strongly believed she would turn me down, but though I wanted to give it a try. I called her and asked her to meet up for coffee.

I wore my lucky shirt, I forgot to elaborate it's a pink shirt with chocolate flowers by john players. It's the most hideous shirt I have. I bought that in my 11th grade and it had some kind of lucky atoms, it brought me luck every time I wear it.

The colony is divided into 7 lanes running parallel to each other, we call them a.b,c,d,e,f,g and main lane. We live in the main lane and Priya in c lane. I picked her up from the d lane and we were just driving in circles.

'hmm.. so tell me what was that urgent thing you wanted to ask?'

'Hmm… ya.. I just wanna ask you something. You could say no if you want to but I might as well go ahead and ask you.'

'Oookay' she said with a bewildered face.

'I'm actually planning to make a short film for applying to a film institute.' I looked at her for any reactions but there weren't any.

'soooo.. I want a female lead for that so would you like to?'

'hmm..okay

I was flabbergasted when she said that. I stopped the car in the middle of the road. I gained my senses back and parked at the side.

'Are you sure? You are gonna act?'

'Yeah why do you sound so shocked?'

'I don't know.. I didn't expect you to say yes.'

Shut up idiot you are gonna burn yourself down, if you say another word.

'Oh really!…why? She said smiling.'

'I don't know for the fact that we barely know each other.'

Please take it back. No self destruction today.

'I know but something inside tells me to do this…' she looked away and took a pause 'there were lot of people who asked me to do a short film but i never said yes that includes my ex-boyfriend. I don't know why I want to do your film.'

One out of ten guys was making a short film in Hyderabad those days.

Keeping that aside, there were pigeons flying over my head in circles when she completed her statement. Why did she say yes to me? Why did she say about her ex to me whom she barely knows? Why? I kept silent with smile on my face. When someone gives me a puzzle and my favorite ice cream, ice cream would liquidize to water. Puzzles are bad for me they freeze my brain to solely concentrate on them and this was the crossword on Sunday morning, Everest of all puzzles.

'Why am I telling this to you?' She said after a long pause between both of us.

How should I know you turned me down for a date and we are barely friends?

'Anyway I have to go. I'll walk my way back home. It's only two lanes away.'

I shrugged and smiled. My brain got froze again it had only one reaction for everything.

'Are you okay you are acting weird'

I shrugged and smiled.

'Okaaay…I'll leave now bye.' She said bewildered and stepped out of the car.

'Bye take care.'

I shrugged and smiled

She closed the door and left. I apologized a million times on phone for behaving that way.

ↄ১ ৪০

Chapter 7

Annoying relatives and dad

Now that I've got everything ready I need to tell my parents to use the house and other things for the shooting. I've sent the information to my dad through Vicky and he approved it. Mom was the tricky one; she can't keep anything inside her stomach. My cousin's friend's sister's son knows that a girl beat me up in my 9th grade. In my defense the girl was huge. Anyway I had to tell her.

'Mom' I mumbled she was busy cooking lunch for us on a Saturday.

'What...' she yelled from the open kitchen.

'I need to talk to you..'

'I don't have time, biryani is gonna get burnt.'

'It's important'

She left the biryani to the maid and walked closer to me 'Okay tell me'

'I want to be a film maker'

'What?'

'You know direction, script-writing...'

'ooh god..' she left a sigh of disapproval 'I thought you were over that stupid thing.'

'No I'm not' I said with a stern voice almost immediately annoyed.

'Okay…your wish.. Carry on.'

Both mom and dad knew that if they said no to it I would pursue anyway. My dad said yes just because he thought that I would fail someday I would join the family business. At least I thought that's in their head.

'So what are you gonna do?'

'I'm making a short film. I'll use the house for the film.'

'Okay.'

She was turning back to leave 'but mom you can't tell this to anyone else. No one needs to know other than the four of us.'

I triggered a time bomb

'You guys always blame me, like I've said everything that goes on in the house to rest of the world. If you guys don't trust me why do you guys say these things to me… she kept nagging and walked away.

Three days later 2 unknown uncles and 1 far related aunt were in my house.

'So you want to be a film maker?' uncle 1 started rattling me.

I looked at him maintaining a smile though I cursed my mom and him a million times in my head.

'Only star kids could be in films like Krishna's son Mahesh babu (south Indian actor)'

'That's an actor uncle I want to be a director' I said clenching my fist, i so wanted to punch that guy.

'Ooh you want to be the guy that operates that machine.' Aunt intervened.

'What machine…the camera, no aunty that's a camera man…D.O.P ur talking about.'

'Okay then you want to make songs for the film?'

'No aunty that's again music director.'

'Actor acts and sings, camera man operates camera; Songs are given by someone else what will you do then?'

'Director is different it's supervising all of them, he visualizes the scene before its on camera' the second uncle intervened and my face glittered as I realized someone has brains. 'I can get you into the film industry.' He said gloating.

I frowned with a smile on my face. I was actually skeptical how he could do that.

'Do you remember chintu?' he kept harping about him. I shook my head with a bewildered look on my face. 'You even played with him in your childhood, he is your Raj uncle's friend's sister in law's daughter's driver. He worked as mohan babu's driver (another veteran south Indian actor). I can put a word for you.'

'I'm flattered but no thank you uncle.' I kept a smile but wanted to plant an R.D.X in his underpants.

I could see my father smiling at my misery sitting at the dining table. Then I heard the bell ringing and opened the door. I saw a tall man wearing a long white Khadi Kurta and a black over coat. He was followed by a couple of other guys dressed in unbuckled formals in dull colors.

I then realized that he is the ex-rural minister of A.P. G Chinna reddy. He is a childhood friend of my father. My father asked all the other guests of my mother and me to shift to other rooms and we obliged. I spared myself from the nut cases by shifting into my brother's room. There was other reason as well; I wanted to eavesdrop on their conversation.

When I entered the room Vicky was lying on the bed nonchalantly.

'Why is he here?' I asked Vicky still surprised.

'Dad is entering into politics some stupid meeting' Vicky said flatly playing temple run on his phone.

'What, when?.. I mean WHY DIDN'T ANYONE SAID THIS TO ME!!? I whisper screamed.

'Yeah right since when are you interested in other peoples life?' Vicky said sarcastically.

'Shut up' I threw an empty water cup at him. He threw that back at me I leaned left and skipped it. He went back to playing temple run on the phone.

'By the way, we went to the camp office to meet the C.M. last weekend when you locked yourself in your room.'

'Why didn't anyone tell me? The scream came out and loud this time

'Shhh…they are right behind that wall we practically begged you to wake up that day. You slept through that time.

'f@*king shit man.'

Chinna reddy lost the elections previous term after winning 3 consecutive times. All it took was a few suitcases filled with cash for the opposition. I started eavesdropping after the small talk is finished between them

'Bhaskar I need to ask you something.'

'Tell me anna,' my father always addressed him as a brother.

'Will you withdraw your name and suggest my name for the congress ticket in tomorrow's meeting?'

My dad without even a gap of micro second said 'of course Anna, not a problem.'

ॐ ॐ

The following Sunday my precious sleep was destroyed by some idiot playing long guitar thing which people call veena and his stupid songs (Thyagaraja kerthana). I wonder why they keep singing the same song Samaja varagamana with different spaces or stretches.. Saaamajavaragamana, Samajaaaavaragamana, Samajavaaaaragamana. I woke up and went to the balcony and I saw Thyagaraja Keerthana written in capital letters. I now know who is the culprit and I promised myself to break his ass into pieces the day I catch him. I know they are playing in my neighbor's house but even mob equipped with flutes and big guitars could be dangerous.

My mother was happy as it was one in the million days when she could feed her son breakfast. My father came out of his room dressed up in khaddar and sat for breakfast. I was intrigued by what I came to know yesterday from my brother.

'Dad are you joining politics again?'

'Hmm.. yes.' He said with his eyes still stuck on the breakfast.

'Then why did you promised to take your name out of the list?'

'Did you hear our conversation yesterday?' he was immediately angry

'Yeah… I overheard.'

'That's bad Surya we never taught you…'

'Yeah I know… but answer me you've spent obscene amount in politics and they had chosen someone else as the M.L.A candidate. You could have won if you fought independently but you didn't. Now they are giving you the ticket and you wanna put it in your friends lap why? I never got the whole point behind this.'

'Neekenduku? (why do you want to know?)' He said in a sarcastic, harsh tone. I've been hearing this sentence since my childhood. It always meant stay out of it. That's the biggest reason behind me being unconcerned by his business.

I was expecting that too. my dad is the biggest puzzle of my life, and every time I ask him if there is any problem or why did he do something he just says that word and I would get pissed. This time I wasn't concerned either I was just intrigued.

I paused and got up in anger.

'Okay ok I'll tell you have your seat.'

I sat down

I'll tell you a secret. I hate politics and I don't want to be a leader where everyone is diplomatic and hypocritical.

'Then why do you spend so much money...'

'Firstly if you give money without a motive behind it people will think you are mad. Secondly if you say you are giving it for free there would be hundreds of them in front of your house. This way I could camouflage my motive. Keeping this entire thing aside I can make friends.'

'What's the use when you don't need any of them?'

'Let me tell you one more thing, if you make 10 friends there is no guarantee that all of them will help you when you are in need but 1 of them would and no matter how big you are you always need friends. The only reason why I help people when they need my help even though I don't know some of them is someday you would need help and one of them might help you. That's the sole reason any grown man like me would have new friends.

Suddenly everything he said made sense to me. Even the most arguable stories had reasoning. My mother when she was married to my dad had to take care of six kids, my dad's cousins and nephews. They lived in a two bed room apartment then. My dad took care of them when they packed their bags and shifted to city. He picked a fight with an insurance company regional head for delaying a guy's returns. The funny part is he met his new friend an hour before picking fight for him.

But he is still wrong. I believe I only live once so I rather have ten good friends whom I love and would take a bullet for them then have hundred just friends. Even when you are a young lad you could have powerful friends M.L.A, M.P. or a Minister's sons. Most of them whom I met are jack asses and I happily am away from them. You could have ten apples then have hundred rotten apples and expect ten of them could be good. If I am in a trouble these ten friends would be there for me no matter what, having hundred of them might give you more options to get out of a sticky situation, but my time is big price to pay for that so not interested.

My father was genuinely a nice guy but I hated him. He might be a philanthropist for the outside world but he mulled over thousands, our pocket money, but that wasn't the reason. He sometimes comes home pissed off and he gets it out on us. My father never wore a tie in his life; being sophisticated was not his cup of tea. He had to get the job done by the workers. He always lived close to them. He had to be rough and that's what he is. He managed not to bring that home for 20 years but the age was not his friend. He started swearing at us, sometimes so I grew apart. Vicky on the other hand took the heat and still had been closer to him. He somehow loved dad more than I did.

Chapter 8

The short film...

That was the first day of my shoot. Okay if you are the first time director there are few things you shouldn't do:

1. Do not act in the movie
2. Very important one DO NOT FALL IN LOVE WITH THE GIRL.

I first thought about hiring an actor for the part it turned out no one was apt for the part. We even thought about having one of priya's friends but he was busy. So all the crew/friends told me to act in it myself as I was the one who knows the protagonist character much better than others and secondly me and akshay would have a better chemistry (2nd worst mistake).

I woke up at 5 in the morning; picked up artists, A.Ds, camera, D.O.P; Came home enacted the first scene (screwed it); picked Priya and the second scene (screwed it big time) we couldn't even keep that scene in the movie hideous scene.

I might be a good writer and film maker, but I'm horrible in acting. If only I kept all the energy into studying I would have been an astronaut. In the midst of all this I connected to priya a little bit. In our house we usually eat spicy food, so spicy that all my friends eat two servings of deserts after a meal. Priya and me had lunch together when crew was busy setting the light, and Akshay on the other hand was busy clicking pictures of himself. She was sitting in front of me, I saw her eyes filled with water

'Are you okay? I asked concerned

'Yeah I'm fine, I like spicy…'she sneezed.

'Yes but your nose is repellant to spicy food.'

'Shut up… can I have some more curry aunty.' She asked the maid politely gasping.

'No way, your eyes would burst with tears if you have more.' I protested and tried to snatch the curry bowl.

She leaped at the bowl before I could and served it herself. She was as cute as a eight year old kid.

'Does your mom make spicy food?'

'No way, my mom measures everything, healthy food.' She said rolling her eyes 'but I love spicy food, I always have it outside. I rarely eat food at my place.'

'You can have it here now; my mom makes the spiciest food.' I smiled

She smiled and nodded her head.

The next few days I took a break to train my actors. Akshay got into the groove pretty quick but Priya on the other hand was Rajnikanth's Chitti in the movie Robot. I realize now that the reason behind that was I played a careless boy who didn't realize the girl's love towards him. Akshay was playing a cupid and comedian which defines him precisely Priya on the other hand was playing a girl who's madly, un-conditionally loved the guy which she never came across till that day. In spite of that she never attended any of the rehearsals except one or two. The Fred cupola and James Cameroon inside me got agitated. They wanted to remove Priya from the film, but they soon realized that Warner brothers are not producing the film so they compromised. I started calling Priya as Priya garu (madam) as an act of sarcastic protest but she took it as a complement and the whole crew followed me calling her Priya garu. After few days we went back to shoot.

We became friends in the mean while. We talked about her family, sister and friends. We started having small talk in between shots when D.O.P is fixing lights.

'I have an exam day after tomorrow' she said with a sad puppy face.

'Oh don't you have to study'

'Yes but I promised I would come to shoot today.'

'Sorry priya I don't know'

'Arey that's okay, I wouldn't have passed anyway....' she winked 'There is this R.K. Sharma's model paper booklet, I searched for it everywhere but I couldn't find it without that my chances are next to zero.'

'Did you try sultan bazaar?'

'Yeah I tried almost every shop.'

'The camera is ready.' The D.O.P yelled from distance as we went back

༄ ෴෴෴෴෴෴෴෴෴෴෴෴෴෴෴෴෴෴෴෴◯

I went through every shop in sultan bazaar and there are more than 200 of them. I never did this kind of a thing for my girl friends; I wondered why I was doing this for her all the way. I got the book in a small shop in the subway of Sultan bazaar, which might be the last shop there.

I went back to her home called her from my car and asked her to come down. She was shell shocked to see the book in my hands.

'How did you get it?'

'I have a guy.'

'Thank you so much.' She kept smiling 'where were you when you called me it was too noisy.'

I called her from the store few times to make sure I had the right book.

I couldn't tell that I was at sultan bazaar for her book, it's too gay. 'I was in the theatre.' I lied.

'Oh which movie?'

'Ahh…hmm..The…the…The karate kid.' Yes good job I patted myself.

'How was that?'

'Good'

'Who was the actor in it?'

What now are we playing kaun banega karorepati. I remembered something related to Will Smith.

'Will Smith'

'I thought it was Jackie Chan's movie.'

'No…No way.'

When you are wrong you have to be 100% confident that makes it right.

'Really!' she looked away little startled 'I'll watch it this Saturday' she said with a smile and left.

I came back and googled The Karate kid there was no Will Smith not even guest appearance. It was his son Jade smith. I cursed Will for not acting in it; I mean his son was acting would it kill him to do a guest appearance in the movie.

CR ℘

I and akshay were having small talk between the shots and priya walked in. Her phone kept beeping in silent mode, her younger sister/second mother. By the way Akshay was afraid of her too. May be afraid is an understatement. She slapped a guy who is unrealistically huge in public, who happens to be my friend. We men are defenseless against women, so we are afraid of them. From the day I heard this story we were afraid to look at Swathi directly.

'So how was your exam?' I asked her

'It was good, the book really helped, I'm really thankful for that.'

No it didn't, she didn't even open the book. She got drunk on vintage wine bottle and slept but she scored well in the test. She said this to me few months later.

The phone kept beeping and I got irritated. I answered the call and placed it on Akshay's ear. Swathi didn't even let akshay say hello. I could hear her screams and akshay walked away with phone plastered to his ear. Swathi didn't even cared who answered the phone. she was just pissed that priya was late to home.

'just a thanks, I need something more.'

'Like what?'

'Hmm… treat.'

'Sure.'

'Hey have you seen the karate kid?'

'no I didn't had time…'

Don't bother it's not that good.'

We walked passed akshay and priya took the phone from akshay's ear and disconnected the call.

$\text{\small ᘓ ᘔ}$

Her phone kept beeping again on our first date/treat. We were getting annoyed by that.

'Hey can you please throw the phone outside.' I said with a smile.

'You're funny.' She smiled and punched my arm playfully.

Why don't people take me seriously? I wasn't kidding

She picked the call and spoke to her in the lowest decibels which humans can't hear and suddenly screamed 'YOU ALWAYS DO THIS SWATHI LET ME HAVE A LIFE!!!' she said with few tears rolling down her cheeks 'well that should give us an hour.' She smiled and wiped her tears away.

'You are evil, do you know that' I said startled at her performance she smiled and winked

She wanted to go to The Cream Stone ice cream parlour. We did even though I hated it and their special chocolate ice cream. We spoke about lot of things that day. Swathi wanted to be a journalist but was forced to do engineering. Priya and Swathi are extremely afraid of dogs and lot of other stuff.

'I wanna have fifteen kids.' I said trying to finish the disgusting mango ice-cream.

'What!!' she exclaimed in shock.

'Yeah I do, I like kids.' I said earnestly.

'You would be around 45 when you have your fifteenth kid!!'

'I know, I would have my own cricket team in my house.'

'I am glad; I'm not your wife.' She looked away with raised eyebrows. 'Poor girl....'

She kept smiling in silence for a while.

'What happened? Why are you giggling so much?' I asked paying the bill.

'Nothing it's just.. I just imagined you with a toddler in your fifties and your wife with a broken back.' She said and burst out laughing.

ॐ   ॐ

We had fun, after haseena she was the one I felt who is genuine and sweet. There was this scene in the film where the antagonist in the movie had to hold Priya's hand and break a couple of bangles but not so tight that it would pierce her skin. We had fake blood for that part. That idiot held it so tight that she started bleeding as the bangles pierced her skin.

I stopped the shoot got her first aid. She on the other hand was acting tough kept saying 'It's not hurting and its okay.' I canceled the shoot, I felt guilty and responsible for that. I asked Priya to have food at my place before she leaves. She got used to the spices now. I was chatting with my crew when I looked at her chatting with my mother. They were both laughing out loud and I was sure my mom leaked the girl beating up Surya story again. She suddenly had twinkle in her eyes when she paused and looked at me for a second. I think that was the moment where my heart first skipped a beat. Ever since that day my heart always skipped a beat.

I was passing by the dinner table and I saw her looking at me from the corner of my eye. My mom started yelling that i skipped lunch but I didn't had time. I had to fix the props for next day's shoot.

'Surya come sit.' priya said in a sweet voice. I looked at her 'Have lunch with me.'

We had lunch together in the middle of all the Havoc. About twenty people moving around, maids, artists, crew, mom but that was something like a candle light dinner as if only we both were there in my house.

℃ ℀

THE NEXT DAY.

Okay that day was like a regular day with shoot crew and the almost screwed short film. We finished more than half of the shoot by then. There was this scene in the movie where Sunny the guy in the movie gets butterflies in his stomach when he looks at sweety (the girl) in a sari. The scene I wrote was sunny goes to her house and sweety was getting ready for a party the lights go out and she walks in with candle in a sari of course

Everything went out exactly as we planned it; except that I was so busy with the other stuff I never looked at Priya until she was in the room waiting for her que to come out.

I looked at her and I can still remember how she looked that day. She was out of this world. Her silky hair was not tied and left open and all I wanted was push that behind her ears so that I could keep looking at her face so cute and innocent that it would make an angel jealous. Her walk was still funny though, she always had that. I smiled for a second but got lost in her eyes, her tulip shaped eyes. Her raspberry lips were tempting, I wanted to kiss them eat them, my tongue would have never left her lips if they were given the permission to enter the slice of heaven. Exactly five steps away from me her lips made a curve looking at me. That's when I noticed she was wearing this beautiful white sari. She stopped a foot or two away from me. Her eyes said a lot of things confusion, inability to act. I felt a skip of heart beat my heart skipped a beat whenever she is anywhere around two feet around me.

'Alla unnanu ra? (how do I look?)' She said her dialogue
'Huh…what?' I was screwed.

I got the expressions right on the first take and the dialogues were blurted out on forty fifth.

Chapter 9

Those three words…

Hyderabad is a place of lots of cuisines but I'm fan of biryani and the Arabic food. I like to call myself a pure non-vegitarian. There isn't a single meal where some animal or its baby died before it becomes my food. I hate urban food too pizzas, burgers don't come under my wish list. Priya made me try vegetarian and it was good not as good as the food in my list though. generally we boys take girls around to places they don't know. Girls take the back seat but It was the other way around with her. She was the encyclopedia of the urban and street food. She introduced Pragati dosa, Krishna nagar tiffins, and grab's pasta and garlic bread, sindhi colony's pizza den. I've never suggested a place besides one or two exceptions.

My D.O.P went to kerala as an assistant for a main stream film. So we took another break. I wanted to meet her every day, she felt the same too. One day she had to go to a friend's wedding in Nizambad (my home town) and I started missing her since I heard the news. She had a tooth gum injury other night when she fell down. She went on to the wedding with that.

We chatted that morning for some time and all I could remember was 'my gum didn't stop bleeding and I miss you' from what she texted me. I took my dad's car and I was on my way to nizambad the next second. First person I called was Akshay.

'Akshay where are you?'

'chepu ra (tell me)' he said yawning

'Nothing lets meet'

'No ra I'm pretty tired, I'm sleeping'

'Ok I thought we will have beer, I'll find someone...'

'Wait!!' he jumped up and yelled frantically 'you should start with that next time. Come to my house. Where are we going by the way?'

'Dhaba'

⊗ ⊗

I went to his house and he came out on a boxer and a t shirt. His theory was we were going to dhaba so we would have the drinks in the car. I swear he was looking like a malnutritious street kid. We crossed the city outskirts.

'Where are we going? We left all the dhabas behind us' akshay asked

'A new one, I'm bored of all the old ones.'

'Where? Goa?' he asked with a wide smile

'No not goa... Nizambad'

'WHAT!!' he yelled in shock he looked funny when his eyes popped out.

'Orey...I'm wearing a boxer and t-shirt; people don't go out of their house like this...

'and yet you decided to grab a bear like this.'

53

'That's not the point, you lured me with BEER!!!' he stressed and yelled the last word 'and why...why Nizambad?

'Priya is over there I want to meet her'

'So meet her she will be back home tomorrow evening.'

'No I want to meet her now, I think…. I think I love her. I want to say this to her yes I will say this…..'

"DON'T EVEN THINK ABOUT IT!!' he screamed in protest 'We are going to their home town and it's a marriage. They will break our bones and parcel them back to our houses.'

I patted him and said 'firstly she is hurt; I need to take her to a doctor. After that I will tell her that I love her.

'Okay do me one last favor keep me a mile away so that I can run away. You know that I'm week and I can't handle beating from the uncle and aunts over there.'

I guffawed and patted him on his back. We reached there at around 1 p.m. she was shocked when I said that I was in nizambad. I kidnapped my doctor uncle from nizambad and took him with us to the dentist, after the treatment I dropped her in front of the hotel where she and her friends wanted to do have dinner

The words "I wanna talk to you stay back for a while… I'm falling for you … I love you" were on the tip of my tongue but they didn't came out. I and akshay crossed a few signals and I still wanted to go back and tell her.

There was silence for a few seconds

'oh screw it' I mumbled and took a u turn I almost bumped into a car in the impulse. I drove back to the restaurant and asked her to come down. There I was standing in a hotel lobby fidgeting. my heart beat went of the roof in that little time she took to come downsairs. I never felt this way since my high school when I was fat, goofy kid. She came down and walked up to me she couldn't talk properly due to the gum ache so she signaled what with her hands

'Priya I want to tell you something…'

She nodded in response and signaled to go on…

'Hmm…yeah…aah…'

2 minutes passed by and all I could get out of my mouth was these sounds all over again.

She stood there patiently smiling

'aaahhh…'

5 minutes passed by and she still had a smile and I forgot words.

'Aah..wait a second' I said and excused myself away.

I called up akshay 'akshay we are going on a drive you have to get down from the car.'

'WHAT!! You want me to get down from the car wearing what I'm wearing.'

'Yes'

No way… not in this life time.'

My eyes fell upon a wine shop right next to the hotel. I bought him a beer and he got down.

on the drive.

'Priya I really love you.' I blurted out as soon as I got into the car. It was easy to say when I'm not looking at her.

'aah…hmm…'

Great now she forgot words.

'I like you too surya…but I…I just… I just need some time to think'

'Okay… at least you didn't say no I'm fine with it.'

I was dancing in my head, if a girl says she needs some time it generally means love you but I want to tease you a little. I picked akshay and we are on the highway in no time. Akshay had a smile plastered on his face and so was i.

'Why are you blushing so much? Akshay asked

'I love priya and I told you what she said.'

'And I love Budweiser. I'm pretty sure it loves me too

'Do you realize that there were at least 100 people who stared at you when you were on the middle of a busy road with a beer in your hands, not to mention wearing just boxers and t-shirt.

'Hmm…things you do for love' he said with a sigh and staring at a half empty beer bottle.

ᬒ   ᬓ

'So you love me but you don't wanna say that you love me.' I said and looked at the digital clock which showed 1 A.M.

'Hmm… yes.' She mumbled

'Can I ask you something?'

'Yeah…'

'Why are you killing me?'

'Hey it's not like that; I just don't wanna have another breakup. I want us to get married.'

First time in my life I was not petrified by that word. 'Okay so you don't trust me'

I know it's ridiculous to talk about that but I wasn't petrified by that word anymore. In fact I imagined that she would take care of my family business, we would have two twin daughters, I would be a retired film maker in my fifties and settle in a hill station. Even I was being silly but I didn't say that to her. 'Okay so you don't trust me.' I said.

'No… it's not that, I just need some time.'

'I don't know about you but my heart skips a beat every time I see you… it just feels right.'

'I know' she sighed.

I realized I was talking like a girl next second. I straightened my voice.

'Okay let me tell you something you are going to say I love you to me by the end of this week… I promise you that'

'In your dreams…'

'Let's have a bet; I'll make you say I love you.'

'Okay it's a bet, what would I get if I win?

'A kiss from me.'

'Stop dreaming kiddo…'

'Okay a kiss or anything in this world except make sure it's in 4 digits, my pocket money ends there.'

'Hehe' she smiled 'the bet is on.'

ନ ଛ

The final scene in the movie was inspired from Romeo and Juliet the hero goes to his girl to reconcile his love after a common fight just like any other romantic comedy.

Priya said all dialogues in the script perfectly. It felt almost she was the character she was playing. Even the part where she had to slap me and cry, she chucked me so hard that I was about to cry. When she cried it felt real. The final dialogue of the movie was I love you. She didn't say that.

I planned my last scene in my grandmother's house so everyone in the crew, my mom, relatives, grandparents were sneaking behind the trees and walls waiting for her dialogue.

'Come on it's your dialogue.' I mumbled after my dialogue.

'I won't say those words.' She mumbled too.

'SAY THE DIALOGUE ITS 1 A.M.!!!'D.O.P yelled from the distance didn't know what was going on. The last shot was a long shot, and the camera was placed on the opposite building.

'Okay ONE LAST, ONE MORE.' I shouted back.

'I love you… I really do.' I said the dialogue forth time.

'I won't say those words.'

'I leaned forward and kissed her on the forehead. That was our first kiss

Chapter 10

The ends and
the new beginnings

Yes she said I love you but not that week. A week later she went on a trip to Chennai. She said I love you right after she returned from the trip.. We kissed in the (A) lane of the colony and it was awesome. Those were the times when mango people had privacy every car was tinted mine was totally tinted. People would need x-ray glasses to look inside.

Some people say making out means sex but I personally say making out is as far as second base. That's everything above the waist if I want to say sex I would say sex or to sound better for girls "make love"

We kissed frequently in my car. Funny thing, it always rained when we went out it was really romantic. There was no lust in my head. Generally I would "make love" by the end of third date sometimes before that, but with her I was in no hurry. I loved the first base with her. I was so busy with the kisses, and hugs I never had time to move up to the second base. I loved holding her in my arms it never felt so good before.

I know I sound like a girl but it's true. Anyway we went over board to second base once in the second week. I felt she was not liking it and i stopped.

'Sorry I just want to be in my limits. I want to do it on our night' she said sitting in my lap and brushing through my hair with her fingers. 'It's just that I'm a little old school at heart.'

'So you never did this before?' I asked startled

She shook her head from left to right and said "you?'

Fuck she is a virgin

'No I never did it'

I just remembered how it made me feel when my first girl friend said that she had it a few times before me. It felt like shit and it burned me a little too. I don't want the love of my life to have the same feeling. So although I had sex on an average of twice a day I said that. All these things just zapped through my head in that split second.

We postponed making love to our wedding night,

I am not proud of this but I dumped a girl just because she said no to have sex with me a couple of times in my adolescent years but Priya was my love. Where ever we go movie, dinner, lunch we took a few extra rounds in the car around the block. I had to stop the car at a few places just to kiss and make out with her.

In fact if we went for dinner it might take an hour but we used to drive round in circles and stop in front of her house making out for two hours. We both used to lose track of time, with her hours were not enough I wanted days years and centuries.

Generally it was girls who complain that we are not giving time, here it was different. I was complaining and she never did. After all we only had 24 hours in a day. Then one day swathi came to know about us. It wasn't so hard though as Priya kept blushing ever since she stepped into the house after that day. Priya wanted me to meet swathi I objected, begged, protested but nothing worked so I wore my lucky shirt. Things went out fine again, LUCKY SHIRT. We had haleem at the Sarvi and we were heading back.

'Sunny let's make a pit stop at central, I need to pick a dress over there.' Priya said, Sunny is my pet name my mom leaked it.

'Don't tell me that it's the dress you saw yesterday!!' Swathi cried out from the back seat.

'Yes it is Swathi mom said I can buy it.'

'You are not buying it. we both share our dresses and you are not buying that hideous dress!! Swathi stressed the last word mockingly.

'Yes I am' priya yelled at her.

'Ok let's show that dress to surya he will decide.'

at central mall swathi showed the dress to me. Swathi looked at it sarcastically and rolled her eyes. Priya showed it to me with a twinkle in her eyes and a smile of a little girl. I was screwed if I go with Swathi, priya would get upset. If I go with Priya Swathi would think I'm a suck up on the first day. Frankly speaking the dress was hideous. It was two or three designs mixed and stitched. I don't know why Priya was so excited.

'The dress doesn't look that good.' I mumbled

'See... even he has a good fashion sense.'

'No don't mistake me to have that attribute.' I smiled

Priya made a puppy face and looked down. Swathi kept making sarcastic comments about the dress. I excused myself to go to men's room.

I dropped them back at home and asked Priya to wait for a few minutes in the car. Swathi walked away into her house I took the cover out and gave it to her. I wasted an entire afternoon in search of a 100 rupee book because of her puppy eyes, the dress was not bigger than that so I bought her… it still looked hideous but she liked it. That day Priya was reluctant to go up stairs or let go of me. She kept hugging and kissing me. I promised swathi that I'll send her up in a few minutes so I had to push her out of my car.

The future present:

I drove thorough the lanes we made out. The streets which reminded me of all wild things we did. Suddenly there was a smile on my face; we didn't spare the TT flyover and Indira Park in our time. It feels like every part of this city reminds me of kisses, hugs, the breath, the feel of her beside me. Did you ever loved someone more than yourself and also hated that someone to the equal amount. I did…

It's even harder to see our loved ones going through the exact gut wrenching misery which we had been through.

'I want to have a tattoo here that says (HA) HASEENA & ARVIND. Haseena said with a twinkle in her eyes.

"Haseena listen to me have it after two years if Arvind works out.'

'What are you saying? I want to give myself that present.' She was adamant

'Do you know something the affect of love, the intensity of love is the same in people who loved? There is absolutely no difference. Either there is no love, or love in this world there is no halfway. You won't even know when your love turns into madness. I know this because I've been through the same situation. This is madness.'

'I know, I'm already mad about him.'
'Tell me about you, are you still in love with Priya?'
'hmm… no..'
'Yes you are don't lie.' She said with a smirk.
'No.. did you ever loved someone more than yourself? And hated that person in the equal amount? I do.'

Haseena is mad about Arvind and I know their relationship is not stable. It's when its going down we realize how badly we want the relationship to work. but it doesn't matter because sometimes anything from a sentence to egos could take love to its grave. And it was hard when Haseena couldn't see the end and was willing to fight a losing battle.

back to past present:

Few days later Priya's best friends Upasana, Aradhana were having a farewell party. Upasana was leaving to Singapore to her parents for ever. Aradhana was leaving to her home town Vizag in a couple of days. Priya was very close to Upasana and Aradhana.

I've got a call around 9.30 in the evening from Priya. I was busy editing the movie, which I apparently screwed up big time.

'Nana'

'hmm… chepu priya (tell me)' I said still trying to edit a screwed up scene.

'I love you.'

'I know that.'

'no you are not getting it.. I really love you' she started sulking like a three year old.

'I know that too… priya how many drinks did you had?' I said shutting down the laptop.

'threeeee +twooooo+fiiiiiiiive +…ouch don't touch me there.' She said in a faltering voice.

'So you had ten large?'

'hehe.' She giggled 'no dumbo threeeee+fiiiiiive…

'okay and what was that ouch?'

'I… I…I got a bump on on head and upana touch it.'

Aradhana took the phone from her

'Hi I'm aradhana, surya right?'

'Yeah hi, okay now what happened' I asked

'Nothing she fell on a glass table and got a bump on her forehead…both upasana and Priya are drunk.

'Where are you girls?'

'xtreme sports bar in front of city center.'

'I'm coming.'

ℭ℞ ℬ℧

'I walked up to Priya and Priya leaped on to me and hugged me.'

'voh…okay what happened?' I said looking down at her.

She looked up hugging me and shook her head left to right smiling with her eyes closed.

I looked up at aradhana holding upasana while she was fighting to have her drink. 'Let's go' I said looking at aradhana she nodded when upasana screamed 'one more' at the bartender.

in the mean while priya bitted me left chest and a part of my nipple through my shirt

'aah!! What!!' I yelled at her.

'I wanna talk to you privately.' She mumbled with tears in her puppy eyes waiting to roll down.

'Okay okay come on let's go.' I said and took her outside.

We went out and sat on the steps. She came close to me and held my left hand in her arms with her fingers running through mine, sat there silently. Suddenly tears started rolling down her eyes and she looked away trying to hide them.

'Hey priya.. What happened?'

'Nothing… nothing she said tears still rolling down.

I held her face in my palms and wiped her tears.

'Tell me what happened'

'It's just that everyone looks down up on us, just because… just because… my mother is divorced…. It sometimes….'

'Shh…now shut up.'

'I love you.'

'I know.' I smiled.

'I'll tell you a secret…come here. She came close to my ear.'

'Let's do THAT today.'

'Yeah right' I said sarcastically…let's go.'

I took her inside and signaled aradhana to bring upasana out. We walked them out of the building aradhana holding upasana and me holding Priya. I called a friend who stays nearby and gave him upasana's car keys he dropped it at her place and gave keys to the watchman and left.

My car carrying the three Charlie's angels had to be driven slowly. Upasana and priya both were new timers and I had to stop regularly so that they don't dirty my car. First time in my life maternal instincts in me kicked in. I never thought boys have that or at least a guy like me would have those. Every time she felt nauseous. I stopped my car close to sidewalk and held her hair and head tightly. I was disgusted by looking at upasana puking but somehow I was taking care of Priya and i liked it.

I stopped in front of upasana's house. Upasana's grandfather was deaf so aradhana somehow sneaked upasana in but priya was reluctant to let go of me. She was adamant about taking her with me.

'I want to come with you…take me with you' she mumbled with her eyes closed and holding my hand tightly.' Aradhana tried to wake her up or pull her back but she was reluctant.

'Okay okay.' I said 'you sleep for a while I'll take you there.'

She shook her head and kissed my left shoulder still holding it tightly with her eyes closed. We waited for her to doze off into the sleep. She slowly loosened her grip and I picked her up in my arms and carried to upasana's house.

Few days later upasana and aradana left, Priya was very close to them. Girls are generally attached to everything from hair pin to high heels, and they…they were best friends. She didn't stop crying since she got into the car. She was on an I.S.D call with upasana.

'Why can't you just…just stay here.' She sounded like a kid again.

I parked the car to left and try to hold her when she kept pushing me. 'but…why…we…'she started crying. 'Come back…kadu (no).

All I could hear was last words from the other side it's not possible. She threw the phone at the dashboard and started looking out at the window sobbing. I tried to hug her but she pushed me away.

'hey it's okay.' I said trying hard to hold her.

'no its okay…'she paused and wiped tears of her cheeks 'I'm okay…

She finally let go and I hugged her tight. She cried her eyes out. I sat there holding her in my arms.

CR   ℘

Chapter 11

Car trade

My dad wanted to take revenge on me for all the things he had to hear in the walkers club so he removed the tint of my car when he gave it for servicing. There by my privacy was at risk and people could see into my car. There by priya wouldn't step into the car knowing how naughty my hands are.

I went to college and at lunch break priya called me for make-out session. In the gigantic poodle of trouble my eyes fell up on the solution Vamshi when I was in the corridor.

Vamshi is a dear friend of mine. His dad is also a good friend of my dad…..

But right now when I saw vamshi I just saw his car tinted exactly like mine used to be.

"vamshi" I yelled when he was about to enter his class room. I walked up to him "vamshi I need your car ra."

"sorry, I have to meet kitty in an hour.. and also what happened to your car?"

Kitty is his longtime girlfriend from same college.

"nothing its right here" I said taking the keys out of my pockets.

if I say car is not tinted he wont exchange his car with my car.

I wanted to show priya how sexy your new alloy wheels are. I've been thinking about buying a set for my car too.

"Really do they look so cool?" he said, his face glittering like a newly wed bride.

"yeah, besides the back seat of my car is bigger than yours."

"true" he said looking down "wait we are not going out to make out." He snapped.

I shrugged.

He sighed."ok lets exchange."

He entered the class room and I walked few steps away "VAMSHI!! Fyi my car doesn't have tint so if you want to make out with kitty take her into the bushes behind the college."

"WHAT!! SURYA!!" he screamed in high pitch but I was far gone as I ran out of the college."

As I was making out with priya in the car parked on the side of a busy road brazenly my phone was constantly buzzing in vibrate mode in my pocket. I let it be as I've sensed that priya liked the buzz on her inner thigh. Half an hour later when I checked my phone there were 26 missed calls from vamshi.

I called him back and he said he is in the bushes behind the college with kitty and the college security guard caught him

☎☎☎☎☎☎☎☎☎☎☎☎☎☎☎☎☎☎☎☎☎

"Dude how could you make out with kitty in an untinted car" I said smiling.

I bribed the college guard and we are on our way walking back into college. He left his purse in the car morning so he had to wait till I come and bribe the guard.

"I had a tinted car but YOU TOOK IT!!!" He yelled flustered with anger.

"okay cool bro. eventhough behind our own college, That's stupidity."

"Again you told me ITS SAFE!!"

"I was kidding…" I mumbled and looked down.

I was walking slow so fell behind and vamshi started picking something from the ground.

"what are you searching for?"

"Asshole! JACKASS!!" He started throwing stones at me and started swearing.

I ran.

I took vamshi to Dabang movie starring Salman Khan that day he wanted to turn down the offer but he couldn't as it was the first day and getting tickets for salman khan film on the first day is a lottery. Even though he was on a silent protest all through the the first half.

"oh come on I said I was sorry." I said as the interval sign appeared on the screen.

"you know I could have brought priya instead of you."

Actually I asked priya first as I've forgotten that she is in the other party (aishwarya rai)

Salman khan and aishwarya rai used to date few years ago. They broke up and she moved on to a new star of those times. I being die hard fan of salman as much as I would have named my first son salman reddy if it hadn't been priya hate aishwarya rai. Priya on the other hand hates Salman being Aishwarya's fan and wants to name our daughter Aishwarya.

"shut the f@&k up, even I know she hates Salman you told me last week…"

I bit my tongue "but still I brought you that counts for something."

"that means nothing." He looked at his phone screen. "I called kitty about a zillion times she is not answering its all because of you."

"ok lets go get a sandwich I'll buy."

He reluctantly walked with me towards the counter. We were watching the movie at cinemax it has an awesome grilled sandwich, Being the first day of salman's film the place was crowded so the guy at the counter took our seat numbers and said he would deliver the sandwich.

When the sandwich was delivered my sandwich was burnt completely and has an ashy taste and his sandwich was golden brown in color and vamshi was making hmmmmm sound moaning with every bite. i threw my sandwich away after first bite.

"hmmmm this sandwich is so good I could have hundred of these."

"can I have a bite?"

"No"

"come on my sandwich is burnt. Just one bite."

"capital N capital O…NO."

I slapped his hand from bottom. Now neither of us had sandwich.

Chapter 12

Walking with insects

The best part about priya is she knows what's running in my head, That's no matter she's around me or miles apart. I later learned that it's some telepathy, one look in my face or one word on phone she reckons everything in my head. Most of the time I used to accept her intuitions but I lied a few times just not to be rude about her friend VENU. VENU the biggest geek I've ever met in my entire life. I hated him from the bottom of my heart. He being a geek is not the reason though

On a Sunday morning I picked up Priya from her house.

'Hey' she said.

I had a smile plastered on my face thinking about the events from the night she was drunk.

'What…what happened?' she said looking at me and then looked at herself in the rare view mirror.

'Nothing… when you were drunk that night…'

'Before you continue you do know that you make me embarrassed.' She said pinching me playfully.'

'Aah..Let me finish first.' I grumbled.

'Okay sorry carry on.'

'You're really cute when you're drunk.'

'What do you mean?'

'I mean...you were really sweet that day. You were holding my hand tightly; your fingers were running through mine...'

I looked at her; she looked at me longingly, took my hand off the gear rod and held it in her hand with her fingers running through mine. Since that day my left hand was borrowed every time I was with her. I drove a million miles with one hand.

This moment was destroyed by Swathi's call. Priya withdrew from the embrace and answered the call. She disconnected the call frantically and said 'let's go have breakfast with Swathi and Venu.'

'Okay but who is venu?'

'He is my brother's friend.' she said reverting back to my favorite posture.

We went around in circles and after a short make out session stopped in front of Priya's house. We were waiting for swathi 'priya could you please clear the back seat...just stuff all that into the front draw.'

'okay.' She said and started shifting.

She took out my graphic novels and started laughing.

'What?'

She pointed the novels at my face still laughing

'They are my novels.'

'Do you call your comic books novels...' she said gasping and still laughing 'my eight year old cousin has the same copy.'

'Yes they are... they are graphic novels.'

'I have to show this to swathi.'

'No!!' I yelled.

'Say that there are comics and I won't sell you out.' she said with a wink and smiled.

I sighed 'okay they are comic books not graphic novels.' I mumbled

ও   ৪০

She sold me out, WITCH the only time I wanted to kill her.

'what suribabu you still read comics?' venu said giggling like a girl.

Ok douche bag I just met you so shut up.

Swathi didn't get time to comment as she couldn't stop laughing… both swathi and priya have a unique style of laughing with their mouths open, no sound and eyes closed.

Venu looked up and frantically said 'Did you guys heard about WALMART!!'

I saw something in the news the other night but I didn't care. I mean who does about a stupid departmental store on a Sunday.

Wal-Mart is a multinational company…it was founded in nineteen something… blah blah blah. It made billions through just departmental stores… you need to know about this guy Sam waltow…blah… blah!!'

I faked a smile whole time and looked at Swathi and Priya for that same reaction but they were seriously listening to him. I've entered another dimension where geeks and nerds like Venu are scoring girls and jocks are losing. Why the hell would girls correction any human being would like to listen to this crap.

In the end of the history class I heard something about Wal-Mart trying to bribe our political parties to get into

Indian market. I raised my hand like a school kid and said 'It's already there in Vijayawada'

'No there is no way'

'I'm serious I saw that in news previous night.'

It turns out that he was wrong the history teacher was actually wrong it does have a branch in Vijayawada. I googled it just to prove him wrong.

Anyway I met venu the douche bag through them and I also met the best couple Anil and Smriti through them. When I meant best I mean BEST-EST couple I know so far.

I met anil for the first time at IBM a business school at the city outskirts. Anil is a funny, happy go lucky guy next door. Smriti on the other hand is a mature loving caring girl in short Priya.

Anyway here is their love story. Anil had a crush on her since a very long time. He proposed to her in a dhaba loventila right next to the college. I don't know if they ever had a fight or not but they both got married to each other one day in spite of their families being miles apart. A perfect lovestory,

Actually Anil was smriti's junior and I was there at her graduation ceremony. I, Swathi, Anil, Smriti had samosas at the college canteen before the ceremony.

'Anil is wearing red boxers.' Smriti commented as Anil got up to bring plates.

Swathi started giggling and I looked down with shy and embarrassment.

'He's feeling shy.' Swathi gasped and went back to laughing.

I stood up 'I'll go with Anil.'

'no no… sit sit.' Smriti said convincing me to sit. 'agar dikhraha hain toh main kya karo? (what can I do if its visible.') she said nonchalantly.

There was a pin drop silence for few seconds

'It's just woh laal hain.' (It's red) Smriti and Swathi looked at each other and started laughing loudly.

Few months earlier I didn't recognize these people even though most of them stay less than a mile away, but something changed. I became part of an old group. Anil was the best medicine for venu's encyclopedia class and swathi was just a boy trapped in a girls body. Ice colas, grab's pasta, pizza den became hangout spots. Swathi became my sister from sister in law.

The only part I was rueful about was bitching. I hated it but girls have the birth right to do that. Once I felt really guilty when I blurted out about a guy avanthika dated in excitement. Actually I just said "Avanthika also…" but the girls black mailed correction priya black mailed me and got the rest of the part out of me. I decided to keep myself out from these sessions since that day.

On the other side, Priya and me crossed second base so that was good too. I know it sounds funny that I was excited to make out with my own girlfriend but I never felt love in making out till then, there was only one minor glitch, the geek venu kept pinching her or hitting her on head. i know he was just being playful but I clenched my fist every time he did that. Priya always noticed this. As I've said She always reads my mind and so there was no use lying to her.

One day I forgot my phone in venu's car and he browsed through my inbox. I didn't bother as I had no problem with it. I said this to priya and swathi they were worried as he was a mutual friend of their cousins too. Since then he started acting weird. He didn't hang out with us much and passed sarcastic comments, sulking. I hated it.

Priya and swathi invited him to a movie once. I usually pick up priya first so that I could make out till Swathi gets ready. That day was not different, I ate all the lipstick she had on her. We kept the phones on silent mode and when we thought we are getting late we switched them back. We saw about ten missed calls on both our phones from Venu. I reluctantly drove to his house and he took the seat behind me.

'what the fuck I was waiting from the past 10 minutes.' He barked at both of us.

I've chosen silence because all the words in my mouth were not censored.

'we went to the main road..' Priya started faking an excuse.

'SHUT UP' he yelled at her making her trail off mid-sentence.

I clenched my fist, and this time my fist was on its way towards his face when priya held it tight and blinked her eyes gesturing not to. I regret that even today. I get raged if someone comments on a girl who just had a drink with me or someone insulting a friend of a friend. Priya was my love, my first love. I was angry more than anyone could imagine. The only thing I regret in my life.

That day even priya was furious. We avoided him for a little while that worked out in my favor. Priya was not a huge fan of public display of affection, so every time I'm with her in public or even with Swathi I had to be suffice with just looking at her. That month there was exhibition going on in hyderabad, exhibition in hyderabad is a mix of fair and carnival. Food, decorative flowers, carpets, dress material, people along with train passing through the path. Generally I never liked crowded places but there were people all over the place and there was hardly any place to stand, so I held her hand. That day the dull and bright lights felt romantic and everything around us was blurred.

I don't know why but both these girls have fun from bargaining. They bargained for ten rupees at some places. To top it up there were these strategies they walk away a little distance and they expect the store keeper to call them back with discounted price. In the end in-spite of their tricks they saved only hundred bucks from purchases of three thousand.

Coming back to the food. We had veg 65 which is nothing but cauliflower cooked in cheap oil served with red liquid almost as dilute as water which they call it sauce but I loved it because of the company. My stomach was upset for two days after that but it was worth it.

We grew closer day by day. I could live if I see her every day, I need to meet her everyday, I want to kiss and make out with her everyday. It was easy to do all that in the beginning but it became difficult as she started working. Ever since she got a job at google I had to be suffice with the first or second one in a day. She had a night job in google and it was hectic for her. In only few days we realized we couldn't live like that so every night. I sneaked out of the house and picked her up at 1 a.m. in the morning from google. The roads were empty and my car was tinted completely. We made out on the flyovers, streets which would be busy in the mornings. Almost all the lanes in the colony.

One of those days…. in the morning.

"Why the hell does the diesel shows empty you filled it yesterday!!" my father screamed at the driver.

I came into the living room and stood there in distance mulling to confess or not.

'I don't know sir, it was full yesterday.' Driver said his hands folded.

My father looked at me doubtfully.

'How would I know!!'

My father called the watchman upstairs

'Sir, babu (son) is going out every night.' watchman blurted out in pressure.

I was screwed..i made up fake story about my friend's birthdays and no body believed it except my mom. If we didn't get enough of each other we met every day in the mornings before sunrise. I think google should pay me at least million as not once in those days she used the office cab assigned to her.

One day we made out early in the morning at osmania university. O.U. is adjacent to our colony. It's a campus bigger than 100 acres with open gate where walkers came everyday to walk and sometimes people like us in cars.

When we are done Swathi asked us to pick her up from the front gate of the university. We stepped out as swathi walked towards us.

'Hey' she said gasping

'hi' I replied

'where were you guys?'

'walking' priya replied almost instantly

I looked at priya blushing and back at swathi "yeah walking"

'What were you up to?' I asked trying very hard to change the topic. I couldn't stop blushing.

'Walking…'

'You too' I said and burst out laughing

'arey whats with this walking?'

Priya pinched me twice from the back trying to make me stop smiling but I couldn't.

೧೨   ೧೨

Anil me and the girls were going to a movie. Anil and swathi in the front seat, me and priya in the back seat. Swathi blurted out the whole incident in front of him and he started making sentences with that word.

'Suribabu lets go for walking.'

'No anil I can't walk with you.' I said and looked at priya blushing. She was looking like a red dragon breathing fire. I was still smiling.

'Okay swathi lets go for walking tomorrow.' He said and looked back at me for a reaction on my face. I was chuckling irresistibly.

Apart from this priya told her friends and family that the love bites on her neck were insect bites. Her mom went an extra mile and consulted a doctor. She didn't knew that the insect was six foot long. Every time people asked her about the love bites I couldn't stop blushing. In short I was always blushing when she is around

Chapter 13

j,,,,,

I and priya go to the same gym, but we don't go at the same time. I established a ground rule that we shouldn't go at the same time. Her workouts are very small. Sometimes she finishes her workout by the time I finish my warmup. After that she keeps pestering me to go out for ice-cream, chat or pasta.

I was worried that I could become santa clause one day, albeit she broke the rule that day.

"what are you doing here?" I asked when I saw her getting on to the cycle next to the treadmill.

"you've said that I disturb you in the gym so we are strangers in the gym."

At this point I slowed down and was standing on the side bars of the tread mill."now if you excuse me I need to use the tread mill handsome stranger." She said

I stepped down from the treadmill and she stepped on to the treadmill backwards looking at me and fell down on her hands as the treadmill was still running. She quickly recouped and braced herself but other people in the cardio room started laughing at her. Though she wasn't hurt she was embarrassed

"Priya…." I said with a guilty smile.

"she placed her palm two inches away from my face."

She does that as her words don't line up quickly when she is angry, and that means talk to my hand. An over enthusiastic trainer faiz walked into the room following the loud noice and people laughing.

A guy cycling in the corner of the room pointed at priya and said she fell down.

"Arerre lagi kya,(are you hurt?) kya tho bhi hain aap,(its ridiculous) aao mai bolta hoom kya karna. (come ill train you)."

She went out of the room with him and later when I was working out in the hall I heard a loud noise from the aerobics room and priya walked out of the room angry.

"what happened?!!" I asked her.

"nothing just a cockroach. And why am I talking to you?" she said turning her back at me. I held her hand and she turned back at me.

"look I'm sorry besides you have to check the treadmill before you step on it."

'you have to switch that thing off its even written on the notice board, in CAPITAL LETTERS!!'

"Ok, I'm sorry"

'Nah' she folded her hands 'you are not getting off this so easily, I need a VETO.'

VETO is a thing we use to forbid each other from doing or saying certain tthings when the other person doesnt like it, But we decided each of us get only 100 VETOs in one lifetime.

For example I VETOed her from using her disgustingly smelly ayurvedic hair oil in the day. She used all her VETOs on my T-shirts and jeans.

"ok what do you want?"

"I VETO to name our son Salman reddy."

"Ok then Its sylvester reddy."

'I veto that too'

'you cant use the veto twice."

She turned back to walk away and I held her hand again.

'ok you have two VETOs'

Her lips made a broad curve 'ok lets go have pani puri.'

'but I still have to workout.' I resisted, she looked at me with her puppy eyes. 'aaahhhhh'I grunted and walked out of the place.'

We walked out of the gate and there was the trainer faiz standing to my left with couple of his friends from the gym. Priya gave him an angry stare and plugged earphones into her ears.

'maine uske pechey pakada aaj aaah jee khush hogaya.'I overheard him saying to his friend.(I pressed her back today, had fun.)

'Kisko!!' his friend asked.

'vohi priya ko.'

At this point I asked priya to walk forward and lied to her that I forgot my purse in the gym.

Priya walked away plugged into her earphones. I walked towards him.

'arrey surya dad kaisey hain aaj dekha unko market main…'(hey surya how's dad, I saw him today in the market.)

He trailed off mid sentence dew to a loud slap. He was shocked so were his friends, but noone dared to touch me. I looked back to walk away and the whole gym was standing outside looking at us. The slap sound was very loud. Faiz held his cheek and stood there, but when he saw everyone looking at him he tried to grab me from behind. I quickly reacted and punched him turning back with my left hand, but the punch misplaced and landed on his neck. He chocked and fell down. Other people grabbed him and took him away as he was having difficulty breathing.

I was not concerned so I walked away as if nothing happened. Priya knew nothing as she was plugged in

🙏🙏🙏🙏🙏🙏🙏🙏🙏🙏🙏🙏🙏🙏🙏🙏🙏🙏🙏🙏🙏🙏🙏🙏🙏

Next day I came home late as I've bunked my college and went to movies with priya. I saw my father along with a few daily labor from my construction site hitting people with sticks, and the mob ran past my car.

My dad stopped looking at my car and I stepped out.

"nena amaindi?!" he asked furious.(what happened yesterday?)

"what…" I was trying to think when he slapped hard on my face

Apparently when my dad arrived at my house to pay daily wages to the workers, he saw unidentified beefy men looking at our house scattered at several corners. quizzed by their appearances he called one of them.

"meru evaru em chestunaru ekada?" he asked.(who are you, and what are you doing here?)

"uncle aap andar jao yeha pai eak londe ko marne aaye hum."(uncle, we have come here to bash up a guy, please step inside.)

Vijay silently went inside grabbed a thick shovel from a worker and started walking back to him. Daily labor who were around 15 people followed him outside.

"kisko marna hain aapko?" vijay asked with no change in his facial expression except his eyes flustered.

Everyone of faiz's friends gathered and faiz who is a coward standing away from the house now came forward and stood in front of vijay. Just when he uttered the word surya vijay turned red with anger and started hitting people. Though the mob ran away I had my dad's fingers printed on my cheek. A small nail pierced into his hand and blood started oozing out profousely as my dad was diabetic and his bp was high. I quickly got him into the car and took him to the hospital. Our family doctor said nothing to worry, gave him T.T. and plastered his hand.

He took me away from my dad and said "your father has high B.P. don't let him do whatever he did today ever again. Its not good for his heart."

He went back to my father in consultation room and said "vijay you should stop eating sweets. Your sugar level is high"

"Hmmmm mmm mmm" he grunted

We drove back home silently. My father was angry and I was worried seeing how vulnerable he is. That's the day I learned that my father was not invincible and it made me week.

The next day when I went to the gym the whole place was looking at me. Priya was standing in one corner warming up as she was brooding for not telling her about the incident. Apparently she found out when her friend from the same gym called her to ask about the incident.

So she was angry that I got into a fight and not telling her about it and the way he had to hear it from the street.

I pleaded her and when that didn't work, I held her hand and dragged her out.

When we were out and no one was watching she bit my hand and I left her out of pain. She turned away and walked towards the gate.

'ok listen PLEASE!!." I yelled and she finally stopped and looked at me.

'I am sorry, you know I had no choice.'

'no you had a choice, you could have walked away like I did.'

'NO I DIDN'T!!. Look I get pissed if someone touched you, that's it. I cant take it anyone in this world should maintain ONE ARM DISTANCE FROM YOU.'I said and looked away.

I looked at her and she was smiling with her hands folded.

"what!!" I asked smiling.

"nothing you are J...A Big J."

"whats J?"

"Short for Jealous."

"I'm not."

"you are."

My junior from the college walked in through the gate...I smiled at her and she smiled back. She walked up to me.

"hey, surya right?"

"yeah and you are from my college?"

"yeah I'm rashmi nice to meet you."

"nice to meet you too."

"actually thank you."

"why?" I asked quizzed.

"that asshole did that to me too."

I smiled "its been my pleasure."

'bye."

'bye.'

The whole time she ignored priya and now priya was red.

"what happened?" I asked

"who is she?"

"rashmi I just met her."

"I don't like her." she mumbled

"J......J......"

"I'm not J."

"J"

"NO"

"J"

"no"

Chapter 14

Miss fire....in love

That day was like every other day. I picked priya from her home and was driving to hitech city to drop her at her office. Akshay called her as my phone was on silent mode. She spoke to him for five minutes using just the words yes, ok, and definitely and disconnected the call.

'Surya had it been more than months since you met akshay?! priya said startled

'hmm ... no... maybe..' I said mulling

'are you serious!!!'

I had no time for anyone or anything else. The little time left after priya was stolen by swathi not that I was complaining but I liked their company.

'I'll meet him this weekend for sure.' I said still mulling over the thought that its been so long.

I met akshay that weekend. My parents went out of town with my brother. So the bar had been officially shifted to my place. Akshay casually mentioned that Vamshi was having trouble with his girlfriend. Vamshi was one of my good friends in the group. His father is also a good friend of my father, in fact my father knows his father since more than ten years.

'what happened?' I asked after second drink.

'nothing his girlfriend wants him to talk to his parents. Her parents are looking for matches to get her married.'

'so whats the problem, he has a good job. His father is a really cool guy as far as I know. He could talk to him.'

'I know but he fears his father you know right, remember the time he freaked out when he got a dent on his dad's car.'

'yeah I know but his father said nothing, its only vamshi who was worried.'

'hmm, I know.' he said looking away.

'I'll talk to his father, I think he will understand.'

Akshay's phone beeped vamshi calling...

'Vamshi today we are going to get your life in order.' Akshay said and switched the phone to speaker mode.

'I know whats in your head, I'll NEVER TALK TO YOU IF YOU DO SOMETHING!!' he barked at him.

I took the phone and switched it back to handset.'Vamshi don't worry he is drunk. Ill take care of everything don't worry.'

'okay...i have to go now bye.' He said and disconnected the call.

I took my phone and called up his father. I had his number as vamshi once called me from his father's number.

'Uncle this is surya.' I said and akshay's face lost its colors. He tried to snatch the phone from me 'uncle one minute.' I said and threw him out of the room.

'Uncle I'm Vijay's son Surya, your son Vamshi is very close friend of mine.'

'Yes I remember .. tell me beta.'Uncle said politely.

'Uncle Vamshi is in love with tanya since a couple of years. Tanya is a very good girl, even their parents are well off. If you could just talk to her parents everything would be fine.'

'who is this tanya?' I felt a little rudeness in his voice.

'Tanya ghantashala, you must have seen her uncle. They both went to the same school. They even lived together in bangalore when he went for training.' I actually wanted to say tanya travelled to bangalore every weekend just to meet him but it came out wrong.

'ok I need sometime ill call you back.' He said flatly and disconnected the call.

I opened the door and akshay was standing with his eyes popped out and his mouth wide open.

'I know what you are thinking but that's okay its all taken in essence of the greater good.'

He squatted down and placed his palms on his head. I made another drink for myself and sat on the bed.

'its all destiny macha (brother). All this is meant to be mark my words his father would say yes to the marriage and vamshi would be grateful to us for the rest of his life.'

Akshay looked at me like he was about to smother me to death.

'Seriously ra.. what are the chances of me having a drink with you today? What are the chances of you raising the topic? What are the chances of me having his dad's number? Its all destiny. its all meant to be. I have a very good feeling about this.'

My phone rang with vamshi's father displaying on the screen.

'hello tell me uncle.' I said trying to sound sober.

'what cast are they from?'

Akshay was now intrigued, he was sitting with his ears pressed to the other side of the phone.

'one second.' I muted the phone.

'padmashali.' Akshay said

'Sure?'

'yes I'm sure.'he whispered.

'padmashali uncle.'

'Then tell him its not possible we cant marry him out of our cast 'uncle blurted out in anger.

'uncle its fine but don't talk about this topic in front of him. He would never tell you about her even though he loved her. He respects you so much, he doesn't know that we called you.'

'we who else is with you?' uncle said furiously.

Akshay waved his hands left to right and fell on my feet and kept whispering 'no, no…no..please don't take my name.

'akshay is with me.'

He disconnected the call.

It turned out a dent on the car and his son's affair were not similar topics to be treated equally.

☙ ❧

The next day morning all the phones in my house were ringing at the same time. Vamshi, and his mother were calling me while my father was talking to his father. I woke up when my phone was still ringing. It was Vamshi, I've let the call miss then another unknown number started beeping on the screen.

'hello.'

'Hello beta I'm vamshi's mother.' She said tensed. 'who is the girl you spoke to uncle about?'

I repeated the whole story once again to her.

'HOW THE HELL DID YOU THINK YOU COULD SAY THIS TO UNCLE!!' she yelled and there was a pause

'I'm sorry think of me as your mother…its been more than twelve hours since Vamshi's father had any medicines. He didn't ate anything. What should I do?... Vamshi doesn't know that I know… why did you?…'

'Aunty my logic was simple, Vamshi would have never spoken to you or uncle regarding this. He respects or fears you people so much. As far as I've heard from my dad what I've seen in these four years if that's true, uncle is very soft I thought he would take it very well. I never wanted to cause any disruption in your family.'

'you should have said this to me first at least.'

'yeah that was my mistake and even if I did aunty would you have talked to uncle about this.'

There was silence for a split second.

'It's just that ten years down the line I don't want Vamshi to think I wish I had spoken to my father may be he could have accepted…'

'it's not possible beta… uncle is very well known in the village. Its ok to get married out of the cast here in the city but not in the village. He has a reputation for which he worked 20 years. He is being torn between the happiness of his son and the name he struggled for twenty years.'

'Sorry aunty but you don't need to fear tell Vamshi that he should delete her from his head and he would. he loves you guys more than that girl.'

'I cant say that to Vamshi. Vamshi is my son…I want him to be happy…'she started crying on the phone.

'Aunty that's ok.' I've hit myself on the head with my fist.

'I too have a daughter… I don't want to ruin her life.. I don't want to ruin Vamshi's life.. I'll call you back later beta..'she said and disconnected the call

Things like this make me hate this society. A man works his ass off and earns a place. Society then recognizes him and labels him by cast, surname etc. since then they have to be 'respectful' in the society.

He or his children cant love someone. That's outrageous how can they do that. Love is very big word. They cant even have a life. He still has to work his ass off to maintain that place in the society. The rest of the time which is left in his life is eaten by weddings of perverts, house warming parties of murderers, birthday parties of dick heads who just envy him. It's unbelievably pathetic that he has to choose between his real friends the ones he grew up with, the ones he love and these assholes. Imagine what would he do if there is a wedding of his friend and the assholes he know on the same day. He has to share his time between both when all he wants to do is stay by his friend. In vamshi's case he had to choose between the assholes and his son. Do you think your friends the ones you love would judge? The ones who would are assholes and we don't need them beside us.

I know that my father learnt about the mess I've created, so I started skipping the talk with my father.

On the other hand I've sent the screwed up short film to few film schools in U.S.A as my portfolio most of them got rejected but Miami state university accepted it and sent me i20.

On the other hand I was deeply in love with priya the thought of not being able to be with her made me sick in the guts. I still made myself strong and blurted it out to priya.

'when did you get it?'she asked with a puppy face.

There was silence for a while. The place turned gloomy suddenly.

'when do you have to go?'

'soon… I might have a month or two.'I said and looked down.

'Surya…'

'yeah… tell me.' I looked up.

'please don't go.' She said with tears just about to trickle down her face.

'hey…'I smiled and caressed her face 'okay' I said and kissed her on the forehead.

We became inseparable after that. As if the whole world didn't exist for us. It was her birthday as I could still remember we pinched and fought with each other playfully trying to grab each others attention. We played hit and run in the middle of a busy restaurant like little kids around our table. I know its too cheesy and childish but it was as if we became six year old kids all over again madly in love with each other.

The next day a bitch named aarti who is her friend said I wasn't right for her because I was immature. Swathi on the other hand became our mother and asked us to behave. We decided we would in public atleast. That promise didn't last more than few weeks.

I still hate aarti. I wish she burns in hell.

One day I picked her up from google in my dad's car. I didn't touch her until we are in the colony as the car was not tinted, but I couldn't resist when we were in the colony. We parked the car between few apartments in darkness. I looked at her she looked at me and I jumped on her and kissed her on the forehead, cheeks, then on the lips. I then hugged her and started kissing her neck. I hugged her tight and started sucking the skin form her collar below her earlobe. I took her top off swiftly. We hugged each other and I started kissing her my tongue started swirling around the treasures of ecstasy and she sucked it leaving me out of breath, and then on the neck, collar bone and bite the shoulder an inch away from the strap mark made by her bra.

'no love bites.'she whispered and moaned 'aaaahhhhh..'
'Okay.'

She still started giving me a love bite on my neck. I opened the black laced bra and she took my top off we were both lying next to each other with nothing on the upper half of our body. I hugged her so tight that not even air could pass between us. I caressed her breasts and started kissing her nipple and bitted them one at a time she moancd a little in pain and pleasure. I went down and down kissing on my way towards the naval. My tongue and lips didn't leave a single inch on her upper body.

I came up and her legs were wide. My penis was erect and started ramming her vagina through my shorts. We still didn't loose our pants but I started moving up and down humping her through the pants. Her hand made her way through my pants and held my penis.

I then related to the conversation we had when we first made out. She wanted to have this on our wedding night. I had sex several times before in lots of wild places. This wasn't sex we were making love, an untinted car in the middle of the road is not the place for that.

'I think we have to stop now.'I said and moved away.

There was silence for a while.

'I want this as much as you want this but not like this at least in closed room with a romantic thing all around. I'm sounding like a girl I know but I don't want to remember this as our first time.'

She looked at me with her eyes saying I love you all the while and hugged me hard causing me to trail of amid sentence and said 'please don't leave me ever.' Tears trickled down her cheeks. We hugged each other for less than five seconds in my head but the time passed by hours together. Time always is in a hurry when she was beside me.

CR ℰ

There were days when I use to die for a single glimpse of yours.

There were days when I got lost in the sparkle of your eyes.

And then there were days where you and I turned into two sides of a coin.

Both so right in our distinct ways which brought parallel spaces between two souls

Days pass by, months cross by, years fly by.

Giving up to the love we share

Making our love stronger as we grew;

Out of all the greatest days in my life,

I cherish the days with a hug, a kiss

A smile on your lips, a place in your heart,

You, my greatest achievement,

My love.

If its time that a million accept love every day then its time we could be one in a million

-R.soleado.

I never realized there was a poet in me until that day. She read it thrice and overwhelmed me with her kisses all over my face. She then hugged me and said 'this is so sweet I wish I could take this home.'

I took her arms off me.

'what do you mean I wish I made this for you. I worked hours on it.' I said pissed.

'surya my mom checks my room inch by inch. I cant risk taking this back home.' She said trying to soothe me.

'then leave, your mom must be waiting for you.' I said looking away.

'I love you…please don't do this.'

'Okay.' I said looking back at her.

'Will you save this for me till our wedding? She said with a smile back on her face.

'No I'm throwing it away the moment you step out of the car.'

'No you are not.' she protested.

'Yes I will.'

She hugged me back tightly. 'I really love you surya… you don't know how much you mean to me, and you look really cute when you are angry just like a little kid…'

'I'm still going to throw that away.'

She kissed my cheek with her arms still wrapped around my neck.

'don't say that..'

'I will.'

Before I could complete my sentence she kissed me tight. I laid back on the driver seat of the car and she slept on me with her head resting on my chest. She hugged me tight and said. 'please don't ever leave me.'

'okay that has to stop that's the second time you are saying that stupid thing.'

'I really love you surya. I don't think I can survive if you leave me. Even if I did I would be a walking corpse. Promise me you wouldn't leave me ever.' She said and looked at me.

'what if you say or do something hurtful in future.'

'I wont and even if I did I will say sorry later in fact ill say sorry now a hundred sorrys for everything stupid thing I'm going to do in future.'

'okay you have to stop the sorrys and don't leave me thing...I'll tell you something every time you say don't leave me its plus ten and every sorry or thank you is plus one.

'for what?'

'sex points.'

'Yak grose

'what as if you don't want to do?' I said and tickled her she giggled like a little girl.

'stop it... please' she said giggling

'ok we call it making out points...your score is hundred and ten.'

'that's cheating, game starts now previous ones doesn't count...And what if you say?'

'still it would be plus ten and plus one.'

'no cheating... then it would be minus ten and minus one.'

'So you don't want to make love to me?'

'darling I can't wait for it but I don't want you to have control over it she said and winked.

�☙   ☙

'84'

'no its 85.' I said.

'you are a big cheater.' She said

'no you are.'

'Guys behave.'said swathi

Our voices were loud

'Okay... sorry.' I said and we braced ourself.

Swathi was sitting in front of me and priya and we are sharing the table in mc donalds.

'and whats with the numbers?' she asked. She looked at me like my seventh grade maths teacher, when I failed.

'good question.' With a smile dying to jump out of my lips 'would you like to answer that.' I said looking at priya.

'Ill tell you later.'She said to swathi and looked down at the Mc spicy burger, she kicked my leg really hard under the table.

Swathi always becomes the bakara (fool) in the scene.

This one time she lost her ear buds. So we went shopping Swathi got down and we decided to stay in the car. every time swathi got down I jumped on to priya and stole a kiss and made out. She didn't got her earbuds in five shops but we encouraged her to try fifteen. I guess may be more.

Chapter 15

Chain reaction

It was a Sunday morning and I was having a brunch in my room and my father barged into my room furiously.

'What the hell are you doing!!' he yelled

'nothing I'm just having my food.'

'not that...this.'he waved the letter from the Miami university

Shit he found it.

'That's....that's just a backup university. I stammered.

'Don't lie to me. your mom said everything. So you are not going to U.S.A now?!

'hmm...'I sighed 'yeah.'

'Are you mad!!' he yelled once more. 'You spent a fortune on your short film and then for applying to those universities!!'

'Dad!! Cool down I want to join the business now.'

'yeah right .. I know why you are saying this.. don't think we are fools.'

'what are you saying dad you wanted me to join...'

'yes but I now want you to go and you are not having any pocket money until you are out of this country'

'I'm not going.' I said scornfully.

'then go to your bitches. I'm not giving you a single penny.'

My mom was standing right behind him along with my brother. I stood up and left the house. Since then I just used my house to sleep in the night. I was out all day with Swathi, Priya and gang. I just looked sad and angry in the house. I was still happy inside for obvious reasons. The money I conned in my college days from my father for fake books and assignments were enough to survive for years with a girlfriend like priya.

One day none of us had any money in pockets. I was totally broke so we went window shopping at a shoe store in a mall me, anil and swathi.

'okay it doesn't matter what I try anil you would say its good and surya you would say its not that good.' Swathi mumbled to both of us

I got into the character quickly.

High heels.

'It looks good' Anil said.

'nah..not that good,' I said.

Ballet flats.

'Good'

'ugly'

Ankle boots

'I don't like it.'

'no I think they are good.'

Flat sandals

'nah… I hate those.'

'aah… sir madam wore those when she came in.' salesman said politely.

'ooh…' I nodded.

'lets go.' Swathi said and we walked out of the shop.

We burst out laughing and I almost had cramps in my stomach.

Everything was going great in my life in spite of me being penny less from past five days. It felt like I was high on something everyday with her, smiling for no reason. She acted like ecstasy on me but I never imagined all this was coming to an end.

The day had come where I had to get brownie points from her mother. One day priya called me up at nine a.m. which was not my regular wakeup time…

'hmm..' I croaked in sleep answering the call.

'you're still sleeping?!!' priya bellowed at me.

'yeah…why? I said rubbing my eyes.

'listen get up nana and get ready.'

'Why? We will meet after an hour.'

'Shut up.. we are not meeting today. I'm going out with my office friends.'

I got up from bed furious and yelled 'what the f!@k!! all you get is one weekend and you want to spend that with your friends. You always do this… last week it was some girls wedding.'

'shh don't say that nana.. that girl is my best friend and today is the last day I promise later I'll give all my weekends to you. I promise.' Her lips are made of sugar it's hard to yell at her when she so sweet to you.

'okay.' I said like a little kid grumbling.

'Now get up and get ready.'

'why you are not meeting me anyway..'still grumbling

'nana…shhh…mom wants someone to take her to my aunt's house. I said you are free today. swathi will be there to give you company.

'so I have to be your driver to have sex with you.'

'hmm yes… I would love to have sex with my fat driver.'

'What!! Im not fat!! I screamed and looked down at my pouch.

'hehe…you are fatty.. my sweet fatty.'

'I'm not I'm just a little over weight and its all because of your stupid pizzas and pastas.

'that's ok my fatty I love your cheeks and your pouch.'

'shut up… I'll pick your mom don't embarrass me anymore I said and disconnected the call.

I looked at myself in the mirror and I was fat. She wanted to see me in shirts and said no to tshirts so I never noticed. And also I was running after her and swathi so no workouts as a result my abs were replaced by a pouch.

 C3   80

'mom this is surya, Surya this is my mom ahalya.' Swathi introduced us to each other.

'hello aunty..' I said smiling.

'hello.'

After some small talk about me and my family, Swathi and aunty went back to talking between themselves.

'Supriya was so beautiful.' Swathi said sympathetically.

'I know even sanjeev was never expected to do that… we thought they are made for each other.'

I sat there confused as there were no subtitles.

'Supriya is my cousin who was murdered..' Swathi said looking at my perplexed face.

Oh yes the doctor and the nephew of that minister. I remember priya said that to me. She was supposedly very beautiful and her husband killed her isn't it?

'Yeah that's her both supriya and sanjeev are my relatives.' Mom is actually going to sanjeev's house today.

'the family was really rich beta they own half the shops in meena bazar.' Meena bazar is a busy market street which yield more than ten million per month.

'But whats the use aunty. If there is no character there is no difference between a dog and a human being.' I said little disgusted by the word rich aunty used to describe such a guy. 'aunty the way we live our lives is the same there is no difference between me or a driver who works for me.. I listen to songs on my iPhone where. when he does it in his china phone. I sleep on a bed he sleeps on a cot laid on the ground. There might be a little difference in the comfort I experience but it's the same. The higher we go the comfort levels might get better by a marginal amount from here. Money isn't everything aunty. He killed his wife for god sake. He killed her because she refused to share her share of property with him. What kind of a guy does that?' I soon got back to my senses from my monologue.'

'I understand beta but that's how people are.'

And she was going to their house to meet them. I still don't understand people sometimes. We reached our destination and she gathered her belongings to get down.

'From today you have become my friend too along with Priya and Swathi. She said and stepped out at sanjeev's house.

This is one part in people I hatted the most the best way to punish asshole like that would be banishing him from the family. My father used to say this in my childhood that if a person commits a despicable crime like that in a village he would be banished along with his family for life time.

Urban people on the other hand are so developed they sympathize with him for a month of jail time he spent. I hate it when people are good to these kind of people. Even priya's mother and priya.

CR   SO

One day priya was asked to meet a guy her mother's friend suggested to get her married. Priya almost instantly blurted out 'I love surya, mom.' Priya's mom took time to diagnose what her daughter just said.

'priya don't mess up your life. Surya isn't settled yet. The guy whom I want you to meet is well educated and WELL SETTLED!!' She screamed.

'he will get settled mom he just needs some time.'

'you are just blind priya he just roams around and spends his father's money.' She said mockingly

'what does your daughter do? she is of the same age as he is.' Priya shouted back at her impulsively.

Her mother startled at what priya said went into the room with her eyes welled up, and swathi followed. Swathi wasn't offended at what her sister said but ahalya was.

'I never thought my daughter would talk to me like that.' She said with tears fighting to stay in the eyes.

'mom that's ok she is just angry.' Swathi said and hugged her.

'she is not getting married to surya for sure.' She said with a frown on her forehead. She wiped her tears away and looked at swathi with rage in her eyes 'I promise you that .. I'll let anyone inside the house again but not him.

Swathi looked at her mother speechless. She could see that her mother meant what she said.

ରେ ଓ

Priya bring me one guy who would get settled at the age of twenty one?!!' I yelled at priya

That was the first time we fought with each other. It was a chain reaction. Her mother yelled at her and she yelled at me.

'What do you want me to do? I feel like shit right now.'

That's because you yelled at your mother, go talk to your mom.'our tones came back to normal.

'no I'm not going to apologize' One thing women are not capable of is say sorry. 'I cant meet you today I don't feel good.'

'bye.' I said and disconnected the call.

ରେ ଓ

I came home that night around eleven or eleven thirty obviously my mood was screwed up. My mom and dad were waiting for me when I entered. I came in looked at them sitting on the sofa and walked past them when they were calling me. I went into my room and bolted the door.

'surya surya…' they kept knocking on the door.

I got up from the bed and opened the door. 'What/?!' I said scornfully.

Dad was standing right in front of the door, with my mom right behind him.

'surya do whatever you want to do. Im really sorry for what I've said…come and have your food. Ill even give your pocket money tomorrow…'

'I don't want your money don't bug me anymore. I DON'T WANT YOUR FOOD!!' I yelled and bolted the door.

'Surya I said sorry what do you want me to do?' dad said in an earnest voice.'surya surya …surya they kept calling me out for ten minutes continuously and knocking the door.

My dad retired after ten minutes my mom didn't. 'Surya I'm not having food unless you have it. Surya suryaaa…' she was still calling my name for ten minutes and was still knocking the door.

My dad came back at the door after that furious and started yelling 'Surya!! SURYA!! He was banging the door hard now. He then pushed it hard enough once to make a slant from the bolt. The wood was tough so the door didn't break. I got up opened the door.

'What!!' I screamed at him furiously.

'You are either having the food or get out of my house right now.' My dad said scornfully.

I was already in my jeans so I left the house. my mom kept yelling and sobbing but I didn't turned back. My brother woke up from the screams and sobbing he tried to stop me but I didn't.

When I was out of the gate there were tears rolling down my cheeks. I was angry but I wasn't sure on whom I was angry. Priya, her mother, my father or all of them. My tears stopped as soon as I crossed the end of the street.

Chapter 16

Chain reaction part 2

Vijay never felt good about himself since the fight he had with surya that day. 'surya was wrong, he was acting crazy.' He tried to reason his behavior. The next minutes would pass regretting what he did. Its been a week since he ate food without feeling bad about himself. For him his sons meant all the happiness in the world. One day of sulky face got surya the red bike he wanted. Another day got him the white sedan he drove.

He fought the whole world to be where he is right now. Ten years back he was conned for four millions in politics. Five years back the water well drilling industry crashed and got him down by two crores. None of these took him down because he knows that the next day he could get up and bounce back and the best is yet to come, but when he saw one of his children sad and sulky it bothered him. All he wanted that day was peace but time had other things in mind.

I woke up after sleeping less than an hour, on the floor and resting my head on a travel bag of a stranger. I didn't realize that last night but I was sleeping in the middle of a humungous crowd. I walked fifteen kms or more than that to sindhi colony. I still don't remember why I did that. I saw a large crowd of people sleeping in front of a gate of a auditorium. I just slept beside them. Next day there were thousands or more youngsters most of them from the other states shouting ROADIES!! The way back was blocked by these people and the way front looked thin. I moved forward and slept in the auditorium for the reality show ROADIES. It was the first time that they came to Hyderabad.

All I know was their seats were much comfortable with cushion than floor. I woke up in the afternoon and there were about forty missed calls half of them were from Priya and the other half from my family. I called her and she picked me up with in fifteen minutes. Akshay the dick head had already blurted out everything.

'what?' I said with a straight face.

She hugged me tight and started crying. I fought the tears as hard as I can but I was week. We sat there in her car for hours tears rushing down through our eyes. Just to be clear I'm not gay and that's the second time I cried till that day since second grade. She had some kind of power over my tear glands.

Praneeth picked me up an hour later and every friend of mine rebuked for not calling them in the night. I was feeling low and wanted to be alone but I couldn't say that so I said "you guys must be sleeping so I thought I shouldn't wake you guys." Now they started lambasting at me. I was huge so they couldn't hit me but they came really close yelling and swearing.

Dad called every single friend of mine to know my whereabouts. I mulled over everything for three days in

Praneeth's house and went home the next day. When my father asked me to sit down and tell him what I wanted

I stammered my way through 'I love priya and I…..I want….to marry her.'

Vicky slapped his forehead and looked at me dismissively

"do whatever you want to do.' My father said scornfully and left.

My mother later explained that they discussed it already. He is not happy about it but he made peace with it.

Ahalya on the other side started reciting the list of my attributes;

"he is just a rich spoiled brat." Ahalya grumbled.

"he is not mom… he is joining his father's business. What more do you want?"

"you mean construction?" she said mockingly

"no the one in africa water well drilling." She said.

"I'm not sending you to africa. Do you think you can live without us over there?"

Emotional blackmail, she played it flawlessly.

'I'm not coming to Africa.'

I closed my eyes and imagined mother in law changing my fourteen toddlers diapers.

"surya are you listening to me?" I cant leave her.

"what more do you want from me Priya? I left my passion for film making. You've become the center of my life." I said and looked up at her

Tears started rolling down her cheeks. Flawless again like mother like daughter.

CR &O

"dad I want to stay in india. I want to start a business here."

My dad held his head low and covered his face with his palm. He fought it really hard but a smile crept up to his face the next second. Surya reminded him the guy he was named after. He then remembered what happened to that Surya and his face turned dark the next second.

'what are you doing with your life Surya?'

I stood there silently.

'The new building is almost done and I don't have anything in pipeline right now.'

I held my head low and walked few steps away.

'WAIT surya.' Dad called me back

'yeah'

'Dev uncle got some proposition about distribution of garnishing spices go and meet him.'

i smiled and left.

Now do you guys remember the dialogue in om shanti om by shahrukh khan 'kisi cheez ko dil se chaha tho puri kaynat usey thumsey milaney ki guzarish karti hain.' Its all bullshit. Its because of these stupid rom-coms we think that the moment we step out of the house the world would be waiting for us to give the noble prize. In reality the world is as hard as your seventh grade math teacher.

I went through every coffee shop in hyderabad holding the broachers and the sample pieces of the spices. Most of them rejected them. Anil's uncle was also in business so few of them were polite doing that. It was a start up company so nobody knew about the brand. Distribution is a simple business on paper. You should buy the products from the manufacturing company, and sell it to the retail outlets, Shops or in my case coffee shops. Tricky part is unless your product is pepsi or lays nobody wants to waste their storage space. Secondly there is no guarantee that they would pay you even if you do all that.

One guy Chef Adin saw me getting out of my car when I parked it in front of Syala. Syala had an open space and a lawn but small indoor space. Adin was sitting in the lawn and waiter pointed him out.

I opened my bag mechanically and displayed the stuff.

"hello sir my name is Surya…"

"dude are you seriously a marketing guy? He asked flabbergasted

'hmm..yeah.'

'and you own that car?'

'yes'

'the one beside that is mine.'

I looked back and there was a black polo fully tinted with black alloy wheels.

'nice wheels sir.'

'in the mean time another marketing guy came there with other products.

'not interested.' He said without turning his eyes away from me before he could say something. He walked away silently.

'sir I'm not gay. I think you are checking me out.' I was feeling weird.

'don't worry neither am i. I was just thinking what would be your story..'

'Have a coffee with me, on the house' he said and snapped his fingers. at the waiter.

One green tea and a club sandwich later I narrated my story to him.

'You do know that all the big distribution companies hire sales guys like the one who was just here.'

'yeah but I cant afford that.'

'even if you can you might do good after five years or more. If you are not eaten by the sharks out there,'

I looked down silently for a second. He patted my back and said 'I'll have five extra virgin olive oils.'

I smiled and said 'you don't have to do this.'

'that's ok I really need them.'

He left me with my green tea to attend a few regular customers. For few minutes I looked down and felt as if I'm living someone else's life. I looked up and I saw my car parked in front of the café. Priya hates that car. We guys love first cars and women inversely proportional to that. She always hits my car when I say I love you to her, by her I mean my car, my first wife. It was so easy to make her jealous and I loved it.

This wasn't the first time I felt this low. Whenever I did I just imagine myself tickling Priya and laughing like little kids. I had a theory that I would hire some ramu as my assistant to do all my work by then and I would be with her, all I need is her.

Chapter 17

The bottom of the curve

Priya shifted her job from goggle to mahindra sathyam. Her office was fifty miles away from the colony so she took her car. Her boss was khadoos Damini now. She made her work till late hours. I couldn't even pick her from the office now. Her mother on the other end made sure we don't meet. She stopped talking to priya so that made her sad. In the time we steal and meet for an hour or two she was gloomy. Months passed with petty fights. Her mother tagged me as a sales man now, another reason in her list. Adin and a few friends bought those products but it was equal to my pocket money and not even close to the diesel I spent on circling other places.

Then one day on a phone conversation.

'I don't know surya… I don't know what to do.'

'what do you mean Priya?'

'I love my mom… there was no one for us from the beginning just the three of us…me, swathi and mom..'

'so.. tell me one thing clearly..if your stupid mom gets you an idiot will you marry him?' i yelled the bomb ticked off now.

'mind your language and my mom would get a nice guy.' She snapped back.

It took me few seconds to register what she just said in my brain 'great then marry that guy don't come after me.' I disconnected the call.

One week later I regretted and called her few times to hear that its definitely over. We were done, the end.

It's the regular routine of the break up in everyone's life. Insomnia, depression, I loved her more than I thought I did. Its hard for a guy to cry but I was crying every alternate day. just the words love priya or even if I was yelling at someone would open my tear glands. I felt like I've gone through balatkar, correction samuhik balatkar. I even harbored thoughts about suicide few times.

I never liked smoking much all I ever used to have is few drinks of scotch. I got addicted to smoking, drinking and on akshay's birthday I tried weed for the first time. I inhaled a puff and held it inside the way they taught me and a guy passed in front of me so I blowed it out on his face. He turned angry and stared at me for few seconds and left.

I don't know what kicked inside me but I would like to believe it was weed. Akshay 's birthday party was held in the farmhouse in the city outskirts so I walked out of the house and started walking in the center of the road. Akshay and other friends of mine dragged me back inside.

There was a large mob of about twenty or more gathered at one place. Akshay said that the guy who stared at me few minutes back was srinath. Srinath is a mini gangster in Hyderabad and also known for his madness. He killed another gangster who was much powerful than him and gained the reputation he has right now.

I walked up to him pushing my friends away.

'bro I think the discussion is for me tell me.' I said trying hard to stand still.

Three of his friends came forward on to my face

'Do you even know whom you are messing with? Ill kill you and bury you right here.' One of them barked at me.

'brother I just tried to kill myself so be my guest and kill me right now.' I said still trying hard to stand still.

All four of them looked at me baffled and srinath spoke for the first time. Love failure a thamudu (brother)

I hugged him tightly and cried for an hour and the next hour passed with the narration of my tale with the gangsters making the first circle sitting around me. At the end srinath said 'tell her name and we will kidnap her from her house right now He said consoling me.

I love her because she is beautiful as a person. Even Swathi is pretty but I actually never found them attractive enough until I knew them. Its like you could see that they are pretty which others cannot.

I said 'kill me.' In the end. Everyone laughed and I did too for few seconds.

→ □ ◆ ◆ ◆ ◆ ◆ ◆ ◆ ◆ ◆ ◆ ◆ ◆ ◆ □ □ □ □ ◆ ◆ ◆ ◆ ◆ ◆ ◆ ◆

Months passed by and I got addicted to alcohol and smoking. Every inch in this world I lived reminded me of her. There isn't a single place which didn't remind me of her. Even camera, film took me back to those memories. I decided to fly away to australia. I wrote IELTS and applied to few universities by then time dragged me through seven to eight months.

I saw my father growing week day by day. We invited him to check in into a hospital. My dad called an ex-minister and got himself a VIP room at NIMS a government hospital. Its specialised for the heart surgeon sudheer reddy who did successful operations on most of the VIPs in the city. He was diagnosed with three blockages in his heart. The same day I got admission in all the universities I applied.

We were all tensed. He stayed in the hospital for four days and I was with him in the hospital everyday. He got about million calls he switched his phone off after a day. Its funny thing with parents. We never say I love you to them. We never hug them. We wipe the kiss of our cheeks the very next second after they embarrass us, but some how inertly we love them more than anything in this world.

We talked about everything from the doomsday to politics in the world during the time I spent in the hospital. I never asked how his health was just because it would make me vulnerable if he says he isn't feeling good. My father was never confined to walls in his life. He hates lying down. on the third day doctor said there was no need for open heart surgery and he needs two stunts. We were relieved that its not as bad as we thought it is.

My dad's friend read a news about Bio stunts in a newspaper. Bio stunts don't need medicines after being placed in the heart. My dad ordered for those and they said they would get delivered in two days.

He was already sick of the hospital staying there was like prison for him. On the fourth day in spite of all our efforts to stop him from getting discharged he got discharged. He said he would attend few meetings and get back on bed by Thursday and also there was christmas on Wednesday and doctors wont operate on a holiday. He had another reason to skip out of the hospital.

I smoked a full box of cigarettes in the morning but I was still tensed that dad was reluctant to go back to hospital. I decided to go work out to take my mind off. I couldn't but I saw priya there. Something inside me dragged me to her.

'Priya dad is going through heart surgery.' I said when I found her alone in the cardio room.

She looked at me like a stranger and shrugged her shoulders. I turned back and walked away. she left a message on facebook but I didn't want to talk to her anymore.

That day 28/12/12.

Dad got up and went to railway station to pickup tickets for my uncle which he shouldn't have. He drove car himself to a private meeting in spite of my insistence to take me with him. He was reluctant and climbed a flight of stairs in construction site to fifth floor which he shouldn't.

He came home sat at the dining table and asked mom to prepare an omelet for him. Halfway through his meal I asked mom to prepare one for me too. He shared a piece of that omelet with me. He spoke to me about my admission in the latrobe university Australia and other things. He went to sleep after that.

At around eleven he woke up and sat in the living room watching t.v. I went for a walk on the terrace and came back when my mom was pestering dad to give a call to emergency. He was coughing profusely for few minutes. Finally I made a call to 108

We reached hospital emergency ward and I was driving right behind him when vicky was with him in the ambulance. He asked vicky to take care of everyone as he saw the inevitability.

I entered hospital when he took a last gasp of air and let it out and closed his eyes. There were several efforts by doctors to revive him but they were all redundant. All I had was tears, me and my family were shattered.

For the first time in my life I was afraid. Till date I was beaten up by people. I've beaten shit out of people. Me and akshay went to fight a gang of fifty and we weren't afraid. I was never afraid of death, wound, goons, thugs, anything but I was now. That day the courage and the heart I had was wounded may be a part of it died with my father.

I always thought if things went out of hand my father would come for me. Though it never did I had something to rely on. that day I was alone I had a family to be taken care of. I saw my mom and vicky and all I thought was if I had died before in the despair of priya they would have been eaten up by the dirty world around. I tried to be strong the whole day but at the end of the day when me and my brother remembered and missed him my eyes welled up and that was the last day I ever had tears in my eyes. I took my fathers place from the next day and I saw an empire he built for himself. There were lands we never knew he acquired for us. Properties he saved for us, bank accounts which we never knew existed, most of all he had an army of friends.

In the first few days the house was insufficient for the guests we had. All the roads in the colony were blocked by cars parked on both sides of the road. Few VIPs and ministers made it worse by stopping the traffic for their passage. There were thousands of people and all of them had a story to tell. One has my father going on a fight with a pack of goons for his friend and the other had a speech which moved thousands of young entrepreneur in old times. He was well known for the patience and the courage he had. There isn't much difference between me and my father.

Its just that my father had more friends and I was content with few.

Its funny that I never told I love you to my father not even once in my life time. We never do, we find that word cheesy so we rather talk about indian politics or cricket match with them. I was feeling sorry about myself for not spending more time with him. I always avoided him because all he talked about was my future and sometimes he had bad mood.

There are days now when I hug my father in dreams and cry for him to come back. Its very hard to be at his place. Ive learned that in a short span of time.

Chapter 18

Good bye, syphlis and arvind swami

1 year later

Girls have this disorder to think that from the moment a guy says I love you to them, he would think about her and only her but that's not true. We have india vs Pakistan match, college fee that was used for bettings and parties, release of assassin creed 3, nagging fathers, change for cigarettes to worry about so you are NOT the epicenter of our universe. This thing annoys them to the power of infinity. If a guy says something other than 'I was just thinking about you.' When his girl calls him he is a dead man.

Akshay's fate was blessed by the lord for the first time and he got a girlfriend Anitha. I couldn't stop laughing when he told me about the conversation he had with her the other night.

Akshay got a call from anitha around 11 pm

'my parents are looking for matches to get me married.' Anitha said.

'okay then what do you want me to do?' akshay asked earnestly.

'I don't know I think I will listen to my parents and marry him.'

'okay no problem carry on.'

'WHY WOULD YOU HAVE A PROBLEM YOU JUST WANT TO GET RID OF ME!!!'She bellowed.

'Do you want me to come over and talk to your parents.'

'no use, they wont listen don't even think about it.'

'okay then get married everything will be fine.' Akshay said loosing all hope in her. "I will also get married to a girl whom my parents think is right for me."

'I will commit SUICIDE THE NEXT DAY!!....' she started shouting.

Akshay scratched his head and mumbled few swear words in low decibels 'okay let me get this straight you would get married to a guy and I shouldn't get married because you would commit suicide.'

'I should marry him because I cant hurt my parents, but you cant.'

Akshay could argue further but he realized it's a futile effort.

That was the last time when we reminisced together the past and shared alaugh before he left the country. Akshay got admission in California university for masters. I would miss him now that he was not ten miles away. Akshay is one guy who could make demon of hell roll down guffawing. I know that we both are destined to got to hell. The time had come, I looked at him walking into the terminal and realized how horribly I would miss him. It was a part of life which I hated the most.

The next day I got a call from priya to meet me at the café coffee day at the street corner. I was perplexed for few minutes but decided to meet her. I was sipping black coffee when she entered in blue Deccan chargers t shirt and ruffled jeans. She looked gorgeous with her hair tied into a pony tail. I braced myself and looked away when she looked at me.

'hi, how are you.' She said with a fake smile.

'I'm fine.' I said looking at her but didn't smile.

'Surya my mother fixed my engagement tomorrow.' She said looking away and bitting her inner lip. I don't know what to do.' She said and started fidgeting.

I looked at her melancholic eyes. They were sore as if she wept all night.

'Don't worry everything will be fine. He might be a nice guy.' I said with a frown on my forehead.

She looked at me with her eyes fighting back the tears and angry in red.

'fine sorry for wasting your….time.' she chocked and uttered the last few words and barged out of the cafe.

That night when priya left the coffee shop I sat there for a while. I didn't know where I could go. Slowly minutes turned into hours. I called vamshi after exchanging few pleasantries he said he was alone at blues. I some how felt he was going through the same thing I went through. I drove to blues.

Blues is a two floor building turned into a makeshift bar and restaurant. The large hall in the ground floor is where we usually sit. It was empty as it almost passed its closing time but the owner likes us so he usually switches the lights off and let us stay till anytime we want to stay.

It has six cubicles in the hall parallel to each other and the aisle in the middle leading to the bar at the other end of the hall. Only one light was on at the cubicle next to the bar.

"hi ra"

"heeeeey my dear friend!!!" he yelled hammered, getting up to hug me."

I hugged him back and we ordered drinks sitting down.

"so?"

"so…"

He took a bottoms up of the glass in front of him.

"you've ruined my life ra." He paused, I remained silent.

"If you hadn't made that call that day, may be I would have convinced my father. Its you…"

He screamed at the waiter for drinks

"I know, I'm not salman khan and neither she is aishwarya but she was perfect for me. She was the prettiest girl for me in this world. Its beautiful, so damn beautiful to be in love, to love the way she smiles, to love the way she screws up things, to love the way she speaks to me… to witness my heart skipping a beat the moment I hear her voice."

Waiter brought the drinks and he gulped them in seconds, both of them.

"Aaaaaaaahhh" he growled and cringed his face as the bitterness reached the end of his tongue. "I am unable to digest the fact that I lost her forever."

"do you remember when I first met you, you used to say love is sex but I never slept with kitty but now I wish to make love to her once, just to make a memory which would last a life time, to kiss one more time, to hug her one more time, to fill her in me one more time.

Just once."

He looked away for a second and looked back at me.

"Everyday, every minute she made me fall in love with her. There wasn't a single day that ended without a fight and kiss. Now there is no one to fight.

He stretched his hands and leaned back on the sofa.

Until yesterday everything was fine today when I look back I lost everything."

. Moments later his lips made a curve, a lopsided smile

"whom should I blame? My father for not understanding or me for not standing up for my love."

He puked in his mouth and a little on the sofa next to him. I took him to the washroom cleaned him up, paid the bill, tipped the waiter heavily and took him back to my house. It was easy to sneak him back in as everyone was sleeping. That night I couldn't sleep. When vamshi spoke to me I felt as if I spoke to myself. I wrote a letter to priya which I never gave it to her.

An ode to love

I wish you never read this, as I know you don't deserve to.

Life is miserable it always has to be for everyone, but not mine. I was happy until I met you. It doesn't mean I wasn't when you were with me. It means you made me miserable when you left me.

Remember the days you used to complain that I don't call you often or say that I love you as much as I should. That's because I never get to keep what I love. God was never that kind enough to me but I never took you for granted. Since the day you entered my life it has always been you.

It would break my heart if you asked me for a crescent moon or kohinoor diamond because I could never get it for you. I wanted all the happiness in this world for you. I wanted to give you everything you ever wanted.

People say time heels everything, bullshit. Everyday a void in me is eating me slowly an no matter how much amount of alcohol goes in its hard to fill the space. It is eating me from inside. I know I have to be strong but I cant sometimes.

Remember the day I was missing you but you were grounded. I parked my car on the street in front of your house, and you came to the balcony to see me. I come there everyday in the night when I know you are sleeping and wait for you for hours. All the blank calls in your phone are from me even the thirysix on a Sunday.

For 361 days in my life there isn't anything in my life but you. The most beautiful 361 days my life, but now every street, every corner, every place reminds me of you.

Sometimes I dream about us getting married in my sleep. I dream of living a lifetime with you, and I wake up with a smile just to realize it was just a dream.

I miss everything about you from your insane addiction to pepsi to holding your hand tight in a horror movie.

I never thought I would but I even miss the stinking smell of ayurvedic oil you apply on a Sunday

I miss you…

I miss the times we kissed at a traffic signal when light turned red. I miss the times I sweared at the traffic signal for turning green too soon

I miss you…

I miss the way you perfectly fit in my arms I miss you. I miss you sleeping on my shoulder when I pick you up after a laborious day at work.

I miss you...

For all the days in this life time you had to come now. And what did you expect? I would run back into your arms and say I love you, I miss you. I cant live without you, because I do.

I do cant live without you, I miss you.

I just wanted to hug you and say that. I now know how heavy vamshi's father felt

I love my father and he has a bigger place in my heart.

I hate you because its easy to hate you than to love you. You left me for your mother, I didn't.

You don't deserve a comeback after all the times I asked you to be with me.

You broke my heart. You made me go through hell and I came back alive from the hell and now you want me back.

I hate you.

I wish you never read this as I know you don't deserve to.

There was nothing to say than that. I was in my fathers place her mother had already fixed her engagement. So I couldn't go and ask her for her daughter. I couldn't elope as I was in my father's place and didn't wanted to loose his reputation. I might have if my father was alive but he isn't and not to forget her words and her actions. I booked a flight to Africa next week and was ready to fly before her wedding.

future present:

i woke up around 4 a.m. with the humidity in Goa making me sweat profusely. I looked at my right and she was sleeping with her mouth open, but still looked beautiful like an angel just like when I first saw her. Since the past few days I realized she has that habit of cuddling. In the beginning I was annoyed by her habit but slowly I got used to it. To be honest even I like it. So I slowly withdrew from her embrace and walked towards the kitchen. Its my friends house so I stumbled steeping on the creaky wooden floor in the hall. I tried to be stealthy but she woke up too.

'what …..are you doing!!' she said yawning standing in front of the bedroom.

'I'm hungry.' I mumbled with puppy eyes.

She smiled and walked towards kitchen. She was looking sexy in her ash colored deep neck, sleeve less vest with my boxers as bottoms. She tied her hair into a bun and started cooking something in the kitchen.

'what are you cooking?' I asked sitting next to the stove.

'Maggi, she said with a smile.

I smiled back.

'but that's not for you it's for me. You make your own food.

I frowned ruefully.

She giggled looking at my face and we had Maggi in the balcony looking at the sunrise. Beautiful, it was enchantingly beautiful to see her when the first rays of sun illuminated her translucent skin.

Back to the past:

I came home after two years. Me, akshay, vicky, haseena we all were in touch through skype and viber. Akshay finished his masters and was coming on a trip to Hyderabad.

I couldn't wait to meet akshay so I turned up at the airport around 2 am. His parents were waiting for him and I recognized them and I went closer to greet them when someone tapped me from back. I turned around and it was akshay. I hugged him and akshay's family came closer to us. I withdrew from the embrace and carried his luggage to the car. I was pretty sure he would get into his fathers car but he didn't. he asked his parents to go home in their car

I missed him… I missed him to the power of infinity all the time we missed was back. their parents left and we took a u turn and went into the airport bar. I had scotch and he had beer just like good old days. We chatted, and laughed as the three peg glasses and two empty beer bottles lay empty on our table.

'mama listen I'm afraid I have syphlis. He said biting his nails after pouring the last few drops of beer into his throat.'

A waiter came to us to take the next order 'what is syphlis?' I looked at him and asked him being delirious.

'I'm new here I'll ask the manager sir.' He said and walked towards the counter as he thought it's a drink.

We both burst out laughing so hard that the whole place was looking at us. I almost rolled down laughing. We went to akshay's place around 6 am and I slept in his room.

The next day morning we realized that we were thrown out of the place for being loud. We had the dosas aunty made for us and a burp later

Akshay came to me with fear daunting in his eyes 'surya, I'm shitting bricks in my pants a girl I had sex with had syphlis. She said this to me when I was boarding the flight to india.

'what's syphlis?' I asked

'it's an S.T.D ahhh…..sexually transmitted disease.'

I was sitting beside akshay so I moved away little

'I don't have aids you asshole.' He shrieked

'let me find out.' I said and dialed haseena's number.

At that point we were unaware of the fact that her handset is broken and she could lift the call but the call was automatically transferred to speaker mode.

'Hi'

'who is this?'

'your boyfriend Athirath.'

'shut up asshole…. I've been calling your other number since you said you are coming to hyderabad….ill kick you in the nuts…do not dare show me your face…by the way I have to tell you something very important… when are you coming to meet me… come tomorrow afternoon to my college we have half day tomorrow.'

'I'm good haseena how are you?'

'Stop that f*#king sarcasm.'

'listen to me dumbo what's syphlis?'

'Syphlis is an STD do you have it?!' she shrieked

'No I don't akshay has it.'

'I DON'T HAVE IT TOO.'

'Okay people please stop shouting in my ears for a second.'

'his ex-girlfriend has it so he is worried that he has it too.'

'wait a minute,' she said and called me back after 2 minutes. 'ok there must be white spots on the genitals.' haseena asked quizzically. But even I'm not sure about it let me check..'she asked her friend beside her who was a doctor unlike haseena who is just a dentist and calls herself a doctor. 'yeah that's right he should have white spots at…..ahhhh

'do you have any white spots at your genitals?' I asked akshay.

he unzipped his pants. 'don't do it here jackass go to bathroom.' I bellowed.

He came back from the bathroom smiling and gave a sigh of relief.

'no he doesn't.' I said and could hear her friend giggling like a little girl.

He came and sat next to me. I moved away. 'maintain distance till you get it checked by a doctor.' I said.

He leaped and bear hugged me and I scuffled to take his hands off me.

The next day we went to her college. We decided to surprise her and walked up to her classroom and we got lost somewhere in a corridor.

A gang of girls dressed in chudidars and white coats were sitting on a ledge of a window.

'excuse me where is the final year dentist's class room? I asked with a broad smile FYI the girl was cute another reason for my broad smile.

'Yeah these two.' she said pointing towards the classrooms abutting the window. 'and whom do you wanna meet actually?' she said smiling back.

'Haseena ahmed.'

'ohh are you by any chance Akshay?' she asked eyes popped out as if Akshay was salman khan. Even the girls beside her were glaring at us now.

'no he is.' I pointed towards him. Akshay standing behind me wearing oversized t shirt and oversized glasses said 'hi.' Thank god he gained little muscle in California he used to look like a kindergarten kid.

Those girls looked at each other and giggled and we looked at each other amused. They whispered among themselves for few more seconds and said 'haseena is in the canteen.' The other two ran past us and people started gathering around us whispering and giggling.

'Ill take you to her.' She said and we started following that mysterious girl.

'Surya did I became popular when I came back from California?'

'Yeah we asked NDTV to telecast you live disembarking the flight.'

Large number of people started following us to canteen.

The loud clamoring noise of people went silent and whispers took their place as if we were in a movie theatre. We realized there was radio playing in the canteen and the voice wasn't familiar so we presumed it to be college radio.

Haseena was sitting on a corner table with her friends and she ran towards us 'what are you guys doing here?' she whisper screamed at us. People staring at us became weirder as if we were a part of a comedy show. Haseena started covering her face and suddenly a loud voice erupted from the speakers. 'LADIES AND GENTLEDOGS A SPECIAL ANNOUNCEMENT WE HAVE A SPECIAL GUEST WITH US TODAY MR.AKSHAY A.K.A SYPHLIS.'

'WOOOOOOWWOOOOWOOOOWOOW.' Boys started barking like dogs and girls started guffawing and even haseena couldn't hide her smile. Regardless to say I laughed my brains out.

಄ ಬ

'Sorry akshay this is the 100th time I'm apologizing to you.' We met for coffee at a coffee day. apparently we were also unaware of the fact that haseena was co hosting college radio that day and her friend left the mike on as she thought the conversation was funny. 'I swear I didn't knew the mike was on.' haseena said earnestly.

'stop sulking now you don't know anyone there.'I said still trying hard not to smile.

'you don't know that my future wife might be a doctor.'he said leaning forward in the chair.

'in your dreams you would be lucky to get your house maid as your wife.'hassena said, Akshay leaned back folding his hands in silent protest against her....again.

'sorry sorry...'

'doctor no chance but may be a dentist.' I winked with a smirk at haseena

'shut up. Anyway I have a surprise for both of you actually there are two surprises for you. One of them is on the way right now. Her phone ringed and she picked it up frantically and walked out of the coffee shop. She embraced a fair guy with glasses. His hair was nicely combed to one side and he was neither tall nor short. He looked like a geek like the ones who never left a library. It was evident that they both were in a relationship the way they held their hands even after withdrawing from the embrace. I was happy for her and I looked left at akshay he had this enigmatic smile on his face but his eyes spoke everything He was sad like sharukh in devdas. Drama queen, does this asshole like haseena? or even worse DOES HE LOVE HER? WHY DIDN'T HE TELL THIS TO ME?

We met Arvind swami that day. I never thought haseena would fall for a guy. I thought she would be single for the lifetime. For one sole reason she is boring, good, dumb, sweet but boring. Atleast I thought she is until I met Arvind swami. He is the most boring person I met. Haseena Is like a second mother to us who puts her foot down and stop's us when we beg for last drink. Now we had the other one who stops us at the first drink. Yes he is a brahmin shudh desi brahmin.

Chapter 19

The second surprise...

I had goose bumps when I first saw that. I've seen everything in my life so surprise is just a word for me. I first thought that its just a dream. There was priya walking towards me wearing an autumn colored dress and a black belt adoring her flat abs. her hair was tied into a pony tail and I wanted to kiss her pink lips. In fact I took a step forward considering that I'm in a dream and wanted to kiss her before the dream ends. She still comes into my dreams sometimes.

Is she married? Why is she coming towards us? I saw haseena and she was the only person with a welcoming smile unlike the bewildered faces like mine and akshay. What the fuck is going on? I had a million things running in my head and all leading upto one thing. WHAT THE FUCK IS SHE DOING HERE.

I was furious as I relocated the pain she made me go through in me. She barely reached our coffee table and those words came out loud. 'what the fuck is she doing here.?!!'

CR EO

Hi my name is priya…

I loved him… I loved him and so did all the atoms in me. I longed for a hug, kiss, his breath flowing on my neck. It was the world for me. I never said this to him too but I cant stop it right now when he is not with me. He was in Africa five thousand miles away. I broke the wedding and my mother disowned me. She swore to never see my face again.

I stood there on the road for an hour before my friends anil and smriti came and took me to their home. The next day I shifted to an appartment and took the job back. Swathi came to me lying to my mother and gave me few of my clothes and things that I need. Astonishingly surya is a very romantic guy, he wrote a poem and and made a painting of us together. Im sure he bribed someone to write that poem and he traced the painting from an archies comic he reads but the gesture was too sweet. I asked Swathi to bring them too. I called him a million times to talk to him. The phone was switched off

Back to coffee day..

I saw her, I hate her may be hate was a small word for that I've been through deepest parts of hell because of her. Im mulling over this every minute. The more I think about it the more I hate her. May be I love her too little bit or may be I love her more than I think I do but that's not enough. I'm not ready to go through that hell once again. I don't have it in me to come back alive.

I've planned a trip to alankritha resorts in africa. Haseena included priya with us. We fought for an hour last night regarding that and I finally said yes. Though I didn't wanted to see her again.

Me, akshay, and vicky were waiting in front of her apartment for priya came out. She was wearing a white sleeveless dress which looked hot and sexy on her, but it was really short and she never wore this kind of a dress. I knew that she is doing all this to impress me again. Its becomes obvious when a girl tries to impress a guy.

"we have to pick swathi too." priya, riding shotgun whispered slowly to vicky who was driving the car so that I wouldn't hear that.

But I did. 'no way we are not picking her up.'

"vicky don't forget there is only your brother in your team but our team is houseful." Vicky looked back at me and shrugged.

CR ॐ

'God you are still not talking to me?!!' Swathi said looking at me and pulled vicky's shirt from the back seat. 'you tell me if your brother broke up with priya would you talk to her even if she is your friend.'

'hmm no…. I guess.'

'NO!!. so you wont talk to me?' priya asked vicky ruefully.

'yes I mean no I would talk to you.'

"WHAT!!" I bellowed.

'no, I mean yes can I please go home I feel trapped between Afghanistan and america.

CR ॐ

They planned really hard to get us together. They left us alone in the cafeteria, parking lot, swimming pool. Nothing worked and they finally let that go and we played foosball just like old times. Swathi is the biggest cheater in any game. They plotted me and priya in a team but I didn't mind it in the end. I was busy trying to defeat Swathi but she won obviously by cheating.

Haseena said she would come there by herself. We sat in the cafeteria after the game. Haseena was walking towards us from a distance and I could sense from distance that something was wrong. I rushed towards her and she hugged me hard and she had tears in her eyes. She was reluctant to let me go. I asked her few times 'what happened?' but she didn't reply and continued to cry. Everyone else made a circle around us and we ushered her to the cafeteria.

"he...he...broke up with me." She said sobbing intermittently.

my next reaction was to look at Akshay's face and his face was glowing like a hundred volt bulb.

'Its ok he is a asshole leave it.'

'he is not!!' she yelled 'he is... he is the best guy in this world. His father expired and his family members didn't let him know till his exams are finished. Now he should get married by the end of this year so they are getting him married to his family friend's daughter. He doesn't want to hurt his mother anymore. He has no choice."

"do you seriously believe this crap." I said "even if its true who does that? I thought only girls are spineless. This guy is a...." I trailed off when haseena yelled "SHUT UP."

"What did you say surya?" swathi said with her voice raising with every word. "priya left her whole family and was waiting for you since god knows how long. How can you call every girl spineless."

"yeah right… I saw the guy she was about to get married to my watchman looks better than him. She knows I'm better option so she came back to me. She is just selfish. She doesn't love me. She doesn't have a spine." I looked at priya just before I finish the sentence and she had tears rolling down her eyes.

"GUYS HASEENA." Akshay yelled pointing her.

And then the place became eerily silent.

℘   ℘

"Wow you are really an asshole. I said this a million times to you but I really mean it." Haseena said rudely after making herself comfortable in the sofa at my living room. It's been a month since I met her. "you think I didn't hear the great speech you gave at alankritha?"

"yeah I'm an asshole only your boyfriend is the best guy in this world. Sorry correction ex-boyfriend."

"Don't you dare bring him between this." She said with a frown on her forehead. And a finger pointed at me. "I tried really hard to bring sense back into your head but you are…. You. Now celebrate your fall even priya doesn't want anything to do with you."

"who cares?" I said looking away to hide my despair.

"yeah who cares about you?" haseena said raising her eyebrows. "before I leave answer few things. How many girls did you had sex with after the breakup?, and why didn't she dated anyone else since the day you broke up with her? And why do you think she waited for you? She could have found better in her circle. After all you are not hrithik roshan."

"because I'm not a eleven finger freak like hrithik."

"be serious abhi tho be serious."

She looked at me with disdain filled in her eyes and stormed out of my house. I slept early that night without having dinner. I generally sleep in my bed room but that day mom went to my relative's house in the other town. So I was alone and slept in the master bedroom.

I woke up when a hand started caressing my hair exactly like the time when I stopped having food for my bike, for my car, and for various other petty things. I opened my eyes and it was dad sitting right beside me the way he used to. I hugged him and wept. I wanted to ask him to come back. I waited to tell him that I can no longer fight the assholes without him. I wanted to tell him to take everything he gave me back and I just …...I JUST WANTED HIM BACK. But I couldn't say a single word to him. I just wept like a little kid.

"I know nanna (son) I'm always with you." He said knowing everything I felt "be brave, you can handle all this like you always did. I'm always with you and I'll carry you at every difficult step of your life."

I withdrew from his embrace and he wiped my tears. "I love you dad." I couldn't tell you this before and I couldn't spend time with you before I regret that.

"It's ok nanna. Now stop crying."

I tried but I couldn't.

"and what did you say to priya? It's wrong nanna."

"I hate her dad. i really do."

"do you know the opposite of love?"

I was silent still crying.

"it's apathy nanna. Hate is just love gone bad. You still love her don't let her go nanna and get up, have food.

There was a loud noise. And I woke up with my pillow wet with tears and my door bell ringing. My aunt brought lunch for me and my father woke me up on time and fed me taking care of my tantrums like he always did.

I was ostracized from the group and vicky went out of town with mom. I forgave priya. I called akshay and he said that priya and haseena are in karnataka in a town called gadag.

෮ ෨

"Not again" akshay ranted as we got into the bus to karnataka. "why do I fall for this all the time. I'm really dumb." He slapped his forehead

I picked up akshay from his house booked a ticket for evening bus in internet and we are off to karnataka.

"don't act so dumb akshay, I know you like haseena. You think I didn't see the contempt in your face when arvind swami walked in, and do you think I didn't see the smile plastered on your face when haseena broke up?"

Akshay bit his tongue "how do you?... when….? Ok please don't tell her ill tell her myself. Don't tell me you already did?!!"

"no I didn't your secret is safe with me."

"will you guys please shut up." A guy from the front seat whisper screamed "people are sleeping."

"Sorry." we went to sleep.

The next day we got down from the bus tired from the journey. We found an auto rickshaw.

"bhaskara hotel." I already booked a room for both of us.

He blabbered something in the local language.

We looked at each other and back at the auto driver. "bhaskara hotel."

He smiled and said "hundred."

We nodded our heads and he took a circle around the bus-stop and stopped behind the bus stop.

We looked at him perplexed and he pointed us at the hotel. The hotel was right behind the bus stop.

Yeh kya app humko ullo banarey yeh to bus stop ka piche hain!! Akshay started shrieking at him. I was laughing at our own stupidity. I paid him the money and tapped his back playfully. We got ready in an hour and we sat in the in house restaurant mulling over what to say to haseena. Finally akshay called and asked her to share her location. We showed the location to the manager and he arranged a taxi for us and said its at least an hour journey from the town.

On our way to gadag (destination) there were lots of sunflower plantations. We asked the driver to stop at one of the gardens. We jumped through the fence and picked two sunflowers and out of no where a guy probably the farmer of the plantation or the keeper ran after us screaming swears in the local language.

"come... come... fast.... Fast." The driver started screaming at us too.

We jumped the fence and ran towards the car like dogs chased out of a field. The driver was ready with engine running and we jumped into the vehicle and fled out of the place.

I looked at my flower and it was scrambled. It lost most of the petals when we were chased. I looked at it with a puppy face for a split second and akshay extended the hand with the flower at me. I took the flower and hugged him and he pushed me away. "get a grip Priya is near by." He said ruefully. I smiled and scribbled his head.

CR BO

"are you sure this is the place?" I said as we reached the destination.

"there was a huge wedding hall with the name image gardens written in capital letters. There were uncles and aunties dressed up in the ethnic wear and saris. They looked at us like we were animals which escaped from the zoo. Frankly they are not wrong to think so. we were the odd ones in that place. We were in three fourth shorts and t-shirts,

"are you sure this is the place?" I asked

"yes I'm damn sure they are inside."

We walked into the place hesitantly all eyes gawking at us. We smiled forcefully at everyone in the place. We saw haseena and priya sitting in the last row of the wedding garden and akshay pulled my sleeve and pointed at the banner reading Arvind weds keerthana. For a split second I was shattered at the thought of priya getting married to someone, Priya holding someone, priya standing next to someone on that platform in front of us. I felt dead, it's the most dreadful thought in my life. I then know how haseena felt. We walked up to them from the back and priya was holding haseena's hand I tapped haseena's shoulder and she looked at us. there were tears welling up in her eyes but not even a single drop had the guts to roll down her cheeks. Both of them looked at us flabbergasted and haseena hugged me in an impulse and few tear drops found their way on my shoulder. She quickly wiped those tears and sported a smile with melancholic eyes. I could see priya turned her eyes away as soon as I looked at her both of them looked gorgeous in their ethnic wear and light jewelry but priya was much more beautiful and graceful. Haseena was dressed in a haphazard manner as if she had no interest in looking good but someone forced her into the blue sari she is wearing. She had no jewelry and her hair was not done well. Priya standing beside her was looking gorgeous like always in her light red sari with her straightened hair left loose. She was wearing a gold necklace which shined every time some light fell on the white stone of the necklace. Her eyes were red and melancholic as if she had worn out of tears crying all night. She was fidgeting little ever since she saw me. She whispered something in haseena's ear and started pacing out of the place. I looked at akshay perplexed about my next move when akshay nodded his head and signaled that he will follow priya. Haseena sat down and i sat beside her.

"haseena... I said hesitant to ask what I was about to and she looked at me. "why are you doing this?" I finally mumbled it out.

"you are a guy you wont understand."

"I will try me."

"I just....i just want to see him happy and may be if I did I might forget him someday...MIGHT..." she broke into tears with last words. I cradled and held her hand.

"hey be strong haseena... my little devil."

She finally smiled and moved away from my embrace. I saw few uncles and aunties starring at us suspiciously but who cares. I looked at the stage again and he was happy with his friends and family. I wanted to say (he is happy) but I didn't.

"you are really dumb.." haseena whispered in my ear.

"why?" I smiled.

"priya is leaving and you are here dumb head." She smiled faintly

I looked at her silently and smiled

"go get her."

"But"

"no buts akshay will take care of me, go get her."

I smiled and rushed outside and I saw akshay standing in front of a cab. Probably the one that brought them here and stopping her from getting inside. Akshay looked at me running towards them from the other side of the road. A car made a screeching sound applying breaks almost at the last minute before hitting me. I ran towards them priya looked at me hearing that sound and I planted a kiss on her lips after the next two seconds. For me the street was empty the garden was deserted and the world was vacuum for that five seconds. I closed my eyes and we were cradling each other. We longed that since eternity. I heard sound of a whistle and I was damn sure that it was akshay. We opened our eyes and there was a crowd of uncles and aunties looking at us perplexed and akshay wasn't there.

We got into the cab and I took my phone out to call akshay and there was a message from haseena.

-stop the P.D.A love birds and get a room. We are leaving to the city and don't bother we will find our way to Hyderabad, AND SERIOUSLY STOP P.D.A you guys are making out in public since past fifteen minutes.

Okay may be we kissed for more than five seconds but definitely not fifteen minutes.

ભ્ર ૪૦

We landed in Hyderabad but I was in no mood to go to my house. We took a taxi to her house. We entered her house.

"you live alone?" I asked checking the house around.

"no I live with my roommate but I guess she went to office."

I leaped onto her as soon as I heard that and showered her face with kisses

"no…no…no" Priya kept mumbling softly, smiling but still kissing me.

I lifted her and took her to the bedroom in my arms and placed her on the bed. I kissed her again starting from her forehead, her eyes, her cheeks, her lips a little longer my tongue battling with her tongue to take control. Then I came down to her neck and kissed her and stopped at a spot right below the ear. Slowly kiss turned into a hickey. She was still mumbling "noooo" in a tone mixed with pleasure of ecstasy and pain. Though her actions were doing the opposite, kissing my earlobe and her hands running wild on my back.

I took her shirt off and she took mine off swiftly. She was perplexed to see that the hooks of her bra were already open. "when did you?"

"in the hall when I hugged you."

I kissed her neck and came down to her bosom. I kissed them one at a time, and she moaned in ecstasy.

"nooooooo….ooo…ooo"

I kissed her breasts until they are ripe as red and came down kissing to her naval and she held my hand scribbling my hair with other hand and pushing head downwards.

"noooooo…oooooooohhhh."

I stopped and looked at her.

"what?" she said

"you are saying no so I stopped." I winked.

she looked at me furious and slapped my head playfully.

I went down and took her pants off and mine too. I hugged her and kissed her naked with not even air to pass between our bodies. She brushed her hand through my hair and kissed my forehead. I held her by the neck and kissed her back on forehead. I nudged a strand of hair on her forehead behind her ear I always loved to do that and kissed her back on forehead. The world was on pause for those few seconds. I moved my fingers through her lips and down through her neck. She felt a tickle and moved her head slightly but kept looking into my eyes. Then we made love for the first time in my life, I made love to a girl. It wasn't sex it was just love. She had tears in her eyes, at the end though her eyes were closed.

"hey…what happened?" I asked shocked. "am I hurting you?"

"yes you did and I loved it…. Its pain mixed with pleasure and the pleasure is only you." She smiled and brushed her hand through my hair. "yes its painful but pleasure is giving you happiness."

That was her first time.

"sorry." I said feeling guilty.

"I would go through this a million times for you." She said Still brushing my hair.

I kissed her on the forehead "I love you."

"hmm…I don't." she said playfully.

"really?" I tickled her and she chuckled irresistibly.

CR 80

Chapter 20

Home and sweet home...

I woke up next day with sunlight burning my eyes slightly through the space between curtains. Priya was sleeping on my shoulder cradling me. She looked like a little girl. I looked at the room and I didn't pay attention before that but it's a small room. Its an 8/10 room with a small bed old flooring pecked at several places. her closet was very small and it stood to the right abutting the bed. I gently moved away from priya and opened it. She had very few clothes and most of them are old and dull which are worn to office usually by her.

I went to the hall had the same pecked flooring like the bedroom. The paint on the walls was patchy. I wondered why she lived in the place as she could afford a better place with her salary. I went into the kitchen to cook Maggi and there was nothing in the kitchen that's edible. Not even Maggi.

I went out and bought her breakfast. She was miffed because I left her alone to get her breakfast. We had break fast in a single plate. The idli and chutney were mediocre but we loved it. She went out of the room and took her phone with her. I could hear that she was mumbling something from the room. I was lying on the bed lazy. She then came in and pushed me into the bathroom as i was reluctant.

She freshened up and we took an auto rickshaw to jubilee hills.

"Where are we going?" I asked perplexed.

"I'm kidnapping you." She winked.

"You don't have to I'm already yours."

She smiled and air kissed me.

Almost half an hour later we were in front of Harley Davidson showroom.

"Why are we here?" I asked perplexed but she was looking for someone in the showroom.

Moments later a guy dressed in formals came towards us.

"Hello sir good morning." Then he looked at priya "this way madam."

We followed him to the garage and to a brand new Harley Davidson low rider. It is white with black stripes running through the tank, Black seats, shining metallic engine and silencer.

He took the keys out of his pockets and gave it to me. I was awed and perplexed at the same time. I had a thought in my head that she bought a Harley for me when I entered the shop but disregarded it as I know she couldn't pay for the down payment. I stood there with my mouth wide open for more than a minute.

I blazed through the streets of Hyderabad and almost everyone on the street was gawking at me. Why wouldn't they be I had a bike which roared like a lion under me and a hot chick behind me. With in no time I was at our place restaurant. I asked haseena to meet me there to show off a little bit.

Haseena was standing at the entrance with a smile on her face. I then realized she already know about this. We had our lunch and priya walked away from our table in the roof garden as she got a call from her office.

"I love her… I said as I looked at her talking to her boss over the phone." I always did… I looked back at haseena. "I can't believe I missed her all the days."

"you realize that now I knew it since the day you took her name in front of me dick head. There was sorry there is a sparkle in your eyes every time you took her name.

I smiled and looked down blushing. I changed the topic to stop myself blushing so much. "hey you should stop swearing so much or else you would look like a loud mouth in my novel.

"Novel you…" she said and sniggered.

"What's so funny?"

"Did you ever hold a pen between your fingers? Your mom in school days and your girl friends in your adolescent years used to do your assignments."

I folded my hand and leaned back and sulked ruefully as she chuckled harder.

I looked back at priya and she looked tensed and the voice on the phone was getting louder.

"haseena how did she buy that bike? I know her salary would not be sufficed."

she sold her platinum chain which was the only reminiscence of her father. She lives in a shitty place to save for the EMI of your bike. She eats vadapav for breakfast and dinner, no lunch. She works for a horrible boss and a horrible company just because they pay 10k more than the other one. She didn't buy a single piece of clothing other than what she needed and she doesn't have a social life. Also she never celebrated her birthday.

I felt small shock after hearing that from haseena. She looked at her and back at me with a smile. "She loves you more than anyone ever did and more than anyone ever would."

I looked at haseena and at priya standing in a distance. The voice of her boss got louder now and she was hiding her sadness with a smile on her face. Apparently her boss was angry because she was on a leave for a week and she couldn't finish her project in the vacation she had. "bye haseena I'll talk to you tomorrow."

Haseena smiled, shook my hand and walked away.

I stood up and walked up to priya. She was facing her back towards me. I took the phone from her hand. "she quits the job. Go fuck yourself." I threw the phone into a distance. She was startled at the series of events and I held her hand took her out of the place.

We went into mebazz store. Priya struggled for a bit to choose between dark blue salwar and light yellow salwar but chose the blue one finally. She came out of the trial room and she looked out of this world. The blue dress had dazzled flowers running through her deep neck and to the shoulders. There were two helpers standing behind her. I paid the bill already so I asked them to cut the tags right away.

"what's in the cover?" she asked me looking at me longingly.

"The yellow one."

"but"

"I already paid for it… and the manager said no returning policy."

She looked at the manager and he gave a broad smile.

Next stop was the jewelry store and we bought the matching ear and finger rings. She wanted to buy a ring with letter S on it. I didn't let her do that. She was angry for a little while but I finally convinced her to go to footwear shopping with me.

☙ ❧

"Aunty would accept me right?" she said fidgeting.

I was sitting right next to her in my house. I texted Vicky the news of Priya in our house in bullet points. He was on his way back home with my mom. He was shocked at the series of events too.

"Don't worry everything will be fine." I said and placed my hand around her shoulder.

"Mr. Surya don't touch a single atom on my body right now." She said

I took my hand away.

"Now sit there she said and pointed at the sofa in front of me."

The door flung open and mom looked to her right where we were sitting facing each other. Vicky was standing right behind her. She had no words as she was shocked. Few seconds passed which turned into minutes for my mom to digest what was happening. later she looked away and walked into my brother's room facing the front door in silence. Vicky walked behind her.

There was silence me and priya looked at each other for few minutes. Mom was not fond of priya reason being dad against us. She even felt the big spat between me and dad was due to her. Priya not being there for me at my father's funeral was not acceptable for her. In a nut shell she had several reasons.

There was then a knock on the door. I didn't expected Vicky or mom to come out and open the door so I opened the door.

There was Priya's MOTHER AHALYA REDDY STANDING IN FRONT OF ME.

ର ଈ

2 years earlier…

"It's not gonna happen vijay. No matter what happens I won't let this happen."

They were standing atop the hill with no one around and city lights shimmering in the darkness

"Don't give me these lies at least, I know surya's age is not the reason and as for wealth all I have is for my sons…"

"I won't let him take my daughter away from me. You didn't let me have one last look at Surya. I hate you and your family." her eyes welled up as soon as she spelt Surya.

"you are wrong ahalya. You were wrong then, and you are wrong now."

ର ଈ

present day…

"I was wrong I was always wrong." ahalya said as she narrated the whole story to us.

Every single one in the room had tears in their eyes. Vicky indeed was crying profusely. I got up and hugged him tight.

ର ଈ

"That bitch took my dress." Priya said trying hard to smile for the photographs.

"Who?" I said still maintaining the cheese smile since past hour without moving the lips and trying hard not to close my eyes from the attack of the flashing lights.

"Swathi who else?!!"

"You are married can you girls stop fighting now at least i said and glared at her still maintaining fake smile. "Anyway what dress?"

"The blue one you bought me that day. I came to your house."

"It's ok I'll buy you new one."

"No that's special for me."

"You have the next best thing." I winked

That was our wedding day.

Epilogue

Surya appointed sridhar as his manager and he called him ramu. He always had a dream to appoint some ramu as his manager and live life care free with priya. Sridhar was miffed for a while though about surya calling him ramu but the summer bonus made it worthwhile for him.

Priya on the other never trusted sridhar. She suspected fowl behavior on his part so she took the front seat and started taking care of the family business. She replaced sridhar with other ramu. Surya's business quantemplified and the started chain of restaurants in U.S.A. vicky takes care of them after quitting the high paid job last year. Nothing changed in surya's life though he used to take pocket money from vijay now he takes it from priya.

Vicky still has a hard time talking to swathi. Even priya tries to set them up few times but vicky screws it everytime.

Vamshi did his M.B.A and moved out of his house after acquiring a job in delhi. His boss promise him 10% partnership in his new startup company for small price which will manifold in following years.

Kavitha realized she has something in common with ahalya. She liked travelling too. They kept going on tours for every six months. Both had great men in their lives and both lost them. They sometimes faze out of the world around them thinking about them and tears find their way out of their hearts. Surya and priya try to move the worlds to keep them happy.

Akshay proposed to haseena 168th time today. This was the big one; he lighted and decorated the whole charminar and the places around it for this occasion, thanks to priya's debit card which surya stole from her purse for this purpose. Obviously his pocket money wouldn't suffice. She still rejected akshay, may be akshay's relentless persistence would find colors someday.

Surya had to hear a lot from priya that evening but he bought concealed ear plugs on ebay for this purpose. It became as routine for him.

Surya and priya fought for the fourth time when she sold his first car, because he kept calling his car girlfriend. Priya is insanely jealous but she never accepts it. Surya has plans to write his first book for some extra pocket money. May be it won't be such a big disaster like his first short film.